A DEVILISH SATURNALIA

a Hellbound novella

HELLBOUND GODS

ALEXA PIPER

MORE BOOKS BY ALEXA PIPER

If you have somehow found this book without having read anything else in the Hellbound series first, I urge you to do so now since the story of the Devil and his necromancer should be read in order:

THE DEVIL'S NECROMANCER
THE DEVIL'S BOYFRIEND
THE DEVIL'S DEMIGOD
THE DEVIL'S WINGS
THE DEVIL'S LOVER
THE DEVIL'S SATURNALIA

The *Monster Apocalypse* Series follows Rory and his big, blue, and handsome monster. (It's an apocalyptical romcom with non-standard anatomy. You will thank me.)

ASH & STONE
MAGIC & HOME
BLOOD & FATE
RORY & INK *(forthcoming January 2023)*

In the market for a dark urban fantasy story?
Check out *Phoenix Immortal!*
*"I couldn't change that I was…attracted to a guy
I'd watched getting murdered on the subway."*
MOONLIGHT CHERRIES

The *Elvenswood Tales* Series has a bit of everything.
The first three are MMF and should be read in order:

HOLIDAY MAGIC

ARROW STRUCK

BONFIRE BRIGHT

Books 4 to 6 are MM standalones with recurring characters:

SIREN'S LOVE SONG
*(in which a siren meets a human
and assists him in pineapple shopping)*

LEGALLY CLAIMED
*(in which a hangry vampire lawyer secures a
human sex worker's blood donation services)*

WITCH WOLF
*(in which a werewolf finds healing in
a witch's arms; a hurt-comfort read)*

And there's more! Find all of Alexa's books on her homepage.

"The lost aren't safe. They are just... lost.
You're not that, and never will be."
— Lucifer

GET IN TOUCH

www.alexapiper.com

INTRODUCTION

Reader,

I swear I thought I could end this first season of Nelly and Lucy's tale with *The Devil's Saturnalia*, but I was wrong, and here we are.

A Devilish Saturnalia was a very spontaneous thing. It follows Nelly and Lucy to snowy Scotland, and it's a sweet, warming holiday tale that picks up right where *The Devil's Saturnalia* ended. It's an extra that you are getting because I love these guys and all the rest of the characters as much as you do!

And as I have said before, you don't need to be sad about their story ending. Nelly and Lucy will have more adventures together or what I keep referring to as a season 2. Before that, they will both pop up in the next book (or several books) set in the Hellbound Gods universe. I hinted at that before, and once more, I'm not saying here whose book it will be in case you are reading *A Devilish Saturnalia* in chronological order in-universe.

The best way to keep track of when you can get more of Nelly and Lucy is to subscribe to my newsletter or join my reader group.

And now, without further ado, let's get into the story.

Alexa Piper
November 2022

CHAPTER ONE

LIONEL

Persephone's castle was well heated, but it was winter, and I was only wearing the Devil's shirt. I was almost expecting to be chilled, but with Lucifer next to me, his hand stroking my back, the cold simply didn't seem to be able to find me. His woodfire-and-spices scent calmed me almost as much as the two small furballs in my arms. Soul kept an eye on them, but she seemed okay with me holding them for now, and Cerberus, no matter that he was the size of a small pony, did not dare approach. He was keeping all six of his eyes on us though.

Quincey's snake tail was weirdly adorable, and Murray looked up at me with her daddy's blue eyes as if she couldn't quite figure out what I was, seeing as how I had no snout or tail or anything at all a good helldog should have.

The dragon mother walking into the castle's great room without a stitch on her shouldn't have surprised me. In fact, when she did, I glanced to the Devil on my left and marveled that he had managed to put on pants earlier this morning. He was busy giving the new momma scratches on her chin while I held the babies. A string of drool was about to land on the left knee of his black slacks, but Lucifer didn't seem to mind. I hoped that wouldn't lead to him randomly taking his pants off with some flimsy, halfhearted excuse. But no, the Devil would never do that. He would never try to excuse taking his pants off.

"Well, what is this?" the dragon mother said, hands on her hips and looking at the wiggling furballs in my lap with a smile on her umber face.

"Dragon mother," Lucifer said. "Meet Murray and Quincey."

Soul growled proudly, and Cerberus yipped from the respectful distance he had kept.

Tiamat chuckled. "Is that what you are calling them?"

"Seemed right," I said and patted Quincey. He was dozing, but his snake tail had latched on to my little finger, which had to be frustrating: the little teeth were not yet strong enough to break skin, so he could get neither blood nor milk from me. "We should build them a nest or something."

Lucifer grunted in agreement and stood. It meant I didn't get to lean on him any longer, which was disappointing. It was nice to have him share his warmth with me, and counterintuitively, having him close made me feel less naked.

I almost felt like a hypocrite about the clothes when the dragon mother squatted in front of me. Right in front. She had her knees spread and everything as if I'd seen the things between a woman's legs. Not that I had anything against the female anatomy, I just didn't need a close-up. Were there really no clothes in this entire castle?

Never before had the need for eye contact only been more challenging.

"May I have a look at them? Make sure they are healthy?" Tiamat asked.

Soul growled in agreement, and so I handed the two small bundles over, carefully loosening the hold of Quincey's snake tail from my finger. Murray blinked at the dragon mother, and as if the blue-eyed hellpuppy could tell Tiamat was family, she started wagging both of her tails, though without much coordination. It was freaking adorable.

"Yes. Two healthy hellbabies," Tiamat pronounced after giving them a once-over and placing them back in my lap. I thought I'd felt her magic too, but it was barely even there before it vanished.

"This should do," Lucifer said.

Cerberus went over to where the Devil had made a blanket nest next to the fireplace and sniffed it almost like he wanted to check it was safe for hellbabies to sleep in. Lucifer let him and lit the kindling and piled wood in the fireplace until the flames were crackling away.

"Come on, babies," I said and carefully got to my feet. Tiamat's hand on my elbow steadied me.

Soul followed, never once taking her eyes off her babies. I knelt by the nest and put the babies on the soft blankets, and the three of them looked comfy. Cerberus had retreated, his eyes remaining focused on the three of them. He tried getting closer once. Soul shut that right down with a not-at-all friendly growl and a glower, and with a yelp, the large helldog went back to just watching.

"Aren't they cute?" I said and turned to look at the dragon mother and my boyfriend.

The two of them stood one next to the other,

Lucifer smiling like…well, like a kid supposedly would on Christmas morning. I didn't know, really, seeing as how I'd never really had that kind of holiday. Tiamat just looked pleased.

"They seem settled," the dragon mother said. "And I will be just outside for some snowbathing in case they need anything."

"Nelly needs a shower," Lucifer said, but the way he said it made it sound lewd. The way he looked at me confirmed that was probably how he'd meant it.

"Getting clean does sound nice." I looked down at myself. His shirt only covered me to the middle of my thigh. "And maybe more clothes."

I knew that would tease him, but I couldn't help myself. Besides, watching Lucifer's eyes go wide and hearing his Devil noises, the sound of snow turning into ice and breaking with a touch, it was seductive.

Tiamat patted Lucifer on the back. "Remember that the first day after Midwinter is best celebrated with a joining of lovers, so mind your stamina."

Lucifer looked shocked. It was so cute. He stared at Tiamat, wide-eyed.

"Dragon mother, my stamina is divine. I could pleasure my boyfriend all through the longest night and through the first day easily."

"Uhm, no, no thank you," I said but was ignored.

Tiamat's laughter sounded exactly like spring felt, a humming deep in your soul. "Careful, Lucy. Don't be too overeager to assure me of something you should confidently possess."

I giggled because Lucifer a tad self-conscious and flustered was a new-to-me experience.

He turned to look at me. "Babe, are you laughing?"

"What, me?"

Tiamat said something about young love as she sauntered off to get to snowbathing outside.

"Yes, you, babe."

"I think you misheard."

"Mmm." Lucifer walked toward me and pulled me up so I stood in front of him. "I think I can trust my ears. Your mouth, maybe not so much. Although it's a very nice mouth." He ran his thumb along the edge of my bottom lip. "So very nice."

Heat poured down my spine and into my belly, and even lower. Lucifer's Devil noises grew louder, and I had his scent in my nose, anise and cinnamon, flames devouring dry logs.

"I'm not at all using my magic," I said.

He smiled his *Welcome to my home, canary* smile at me.

"That is so very good of you, my love."

And he teleported us. Gone was the great room and the massive Christmas tree with the magic lights spelled to shimmer above it. Gone were the canine residents of the castle.

We were back in our room. Lucifer ran a hand through my hair, paused, and pulled on one of my new ear studs.

I winced, but the pain shot straight to my balls as a wave of arousal, and I whined at the strangeness of being turned on by pain.

"I think you can have a shower after I've had you, babe," Lucifer said, his tone light as if he were considering something utterly mundane, like which color shirt to wear.

I opened my mouth. Closed it again. Then I leaned into him, my arms coming around to hug him close. I couldn't remember ever doing this before, seeking out his warmth like this, but it was still so new, knowing that he was and would be mine, today, tomorrow, always.

"I love you," I said, not quite sure he would hear, but of course his hearing—much like his stamina—was divine.

"And I you, Nelly."

He moved us to the bed, leading me along in tiny steps without ever breaking our embrace, and then he went so far as to let himself fall backward into the pillows.

My landing was comparatively soft, even though Lucifer was firm, but through a stroke of luck, I managed not to impale myself on his rigid cock.

"Babe, are you laughing again? It's not the reaction I had hoped for," he said as his hands wandered down to my naked ass. I had been wearing underwear yesterday, but oh, those days when I was able to fall asleep wearing my underwear. When I'd been able to wear whatever I pleased when I fell into bed. Now, I was either wrapped in sexy Devil or sexy Devil's wings since Lucifer didn't allow me to wear clothes in bed. If I was being honest, I liked it that way, but I really wasn't in a place where I could fully admit that to myself or even say it out loud, so I took the thought and jammed it into the back of a drawer in my mind for later examination.

"I was just thinking your cock is hard enough to poke my eye out," I said, partly because I wanted to see his reaction.

I lifted my head off his chest to see him frowning down at me

"As I said, divine stamina," he said.

"Right. You did say that. I almost forgot."

"Did you?" He flipped us over in one swift move that did something to my lizard brain, which recognized this move as *hella hot*. Probably the scientific term. The way

Lucifer looked down at me, he knew how my lizard brain worked.

"You are correct about my cock being painfully hard," he went on after taking his sweet fucking time to look me over like a cut of meat he couldn't decide to cook or eat raw. "And I need to do something about that." He shifted until he straddled me, then scooted up my body until his knees were on either side of my shoulders, his dripping cock looming right above my mouth.

I started salivating like I was sure he wanted me to, and a shiver ran down my spine. I couldn't look anywhere but up at him, at the very obvious part of him right above me, but also beyond that, at his eyes, sapphire bright and laser focused on me.

He took his cock in hand and ran the already slick tip along my lips. I let my mouth fall open and licked up the salty precum, and when I grazed the head with my tongue, he hissed in pleasure.

"Lick," he commanded, and my mouth fell open that much wider so I could properly run my tongue over his cock and taste him.

I'd expected him to tell me to open and fuck into me. Usually, he'd tie me up for that, but weirdly, this felt even more constricting, especially when he pushed my head back down the moment I tried lifting it to better take him into my mouth.

"No, babe. You'll just get to savor for now. Lick. Yes, that's right, use that lovely tongue."

The appeal of being on my back underneath Lucifer became obvious pretty quickly. The noises he made— those Devil noises—grew louder and darker, more intimate. Hungrier. His leg and hip muscles flexed, and while my range of movement wasn't wide, I could reach up to stroke his ass and thighs with my fingers, something he seemed to enjoy. If he hadn't, he'd have gotten out a rope.

Meanwhile, he was producing more and more precum, and I licked and sucked, the taste of it even more intensely smoke and spices, fire and heat, than his scent alone.

"Very nice, my love. You are doing so well," he praised. "Let me get you ready for your reward. Don't use your magic while I do that, babe. Keep it still."

His magic reached for me in slow and tender strokes. I had to concentrate on keeping calm, but it wasn't painful at all. It still felt like an intrusion, but if anything it was an intrusion much like fucking was an intrusion, and just like fucking, getting cleaned and slicked by his magic was arousing.

My toes curled, and I rubbed my legs together, seeing as how I didn't have the Devil sitting on my knees, just on my chest. He totally overdid it with the lubing up, the ass, and I started whimpering even as I did my best to cradle his cockhead with my tongue.

Lucifer chuckled. "You know I like you slick, babe. Don't you want to be exactly the way I want you?" He pulled his hips back so I didn't have anything to lick and could actually answer.

"It's just a lot. And I told you I'm not a water ride at some amusement park."

He laughed, the vibrato going through my chest and making my balls tingle. "Babe. I swear you are behaving too virginal. That comment was almost word for word out of a novel I read the other day, and in that, it was the virgin who said it."

I frowned. That probably didn't have a lot of effect,

given I was under him and pinned to the bed, but still.

"You can stop with this already unless you want me to reconnect with every guy I—"

Lucifer's growl stopped me cold. "What did I tell you, babe, hmm?"

I swallowed. His intense stare was, well, intense. "Don't talk about other men when I'm in your bed."

I glanced to the side. "To be fair, you started it."

I counted three seconds of silence, before he said, "Is that so? Well, then I must apologize." His weight quickly left me before I was flipped over and slammed onto my belly. "I must apologize for making you think of other men." He roughly pushed my legs apart, and my hole quivered with the knowledge and anticipation of what was coming. "I must apologize for not being clear in my desires." He positioned himself above and pushed into me. Every nerve ending tingled with the sweet roughness of it. "I want you to only think of me," he said and buried his cock all the way inside.

"L-Lucy," I gasped, near breathless.

"Good boy, you're taking me so well. Now, for my apology…"

He fucked into me, hard and rough and *good*. I was pinned again, properly this time, my fingers clutching at the sheets in uncoordinated spasms with each deep thrust. I was hard, ragingly hard, and horny, and I had barely a moment to notice how my body felt about this whole situation before I came, untouched, in hot spurts that only ended in the tangled comforter beneath me.

I heard myself whine. It barely registered above Lucifer's panting, like a racehorse going for the finish line.

"Yes, sweet, that's right, you come for me, only from my cock," he said. His breath washed over my ear and the side of my face, and my body was about ready to lock up—but he was still going.

"Please," I managed.

"You'll come again for me," he said, simple as that.

I moaned. He had to be fucking joking.

"You want to be good for me, my love," he coaxed and slowed although he never stopped. It was confusing, too much happening, too many sensations.

I shook as if electricity were running through me. Lucifer made his dark and devilish sounds, his tongue licking along the shell of my ear, down to my stud. He played with it for a moment, and I whimpered because even in my pleasure-addled brain, I knew what was coming.

His teeth closed around the earring, and he pulled, then readjusted our positions long enough to shove a pillow under my belly. He pulled back, almost pulled out, and with one hand, he started stroking my cock, teasingly pulling the foreskin back and working on the head with his thumb.

After jerking my earring, which made me cry out, he released my ear and leaned right back in to whisper, "That's right, babe. You'll get hard when I touch you, whether you just came or not." He slammed into me again. I couldn't squirm, because my every sinew and muscle was wound taut as a tensed bow, and each jerky reaction was an involuntary one, but I fucking reacted. "Yes, sweet, you're being so very good," he said before kissing my cheek.

The rest of it was a haze of addiction-inducing too much too fast, everything all at once. I knew I came for him, because that orgasm stood out brighter, even if he'd already lit my every cell on fire by then. I knew he came too, after that, because that sonorous moan of pleasure and release could only have come from his divine mouth.

Distantly, I realized I'd teared up at some point, my eyes watering and spit dribbling out of the corners of my mouth, but when he was done, like he always did, Lucifer took care of me. And if I had learned anything these past few days, it was that I could trust the Devil utterly and I was the safest when he held me, so I let him and drifted off into a nap, which I totally deserved.

CHAPTER TWO
LUCIFER

Nelly still smelled like the intoxicating demigod he was, young wine and sun-kissed grapes. I inhaled his scent and went so far as to pull him up so his head was closer and I could sniff his hair. If he'd been even the slightest measure of less well-fucked, he'd have sassed me for it, but I was the Devil, and I knew how to use my cock to shut my boyfriend up—in the best of ways.

At any rate, he was too damn adorable to resist, the way he'd handled Soul's hellspawn, and I quickly needed to get him to agree to a deal that would let me tie him to the bed permanently, maybe with an allowance to go out once a month or so.

I sighed and looked up at the carved wooden ceiling tiles. Of course I was not going to keep him all to myself (unless the opportunity spontaneously arose), and of course his satisfaction and happiness with his life was more important than getting to keep him to myself. It was an unspoken deal when one loved another, and no one had warned me that love would be like that.

I ran my hand up his thigh, and as if he were just waiting for my cue, even in sleep, Nelly curled into me.

I shifted a little to the side and unfolded first one wing then turned to unfold the other so I could wrap him in my feathers. Through the touch, I felt his mind react and relax, just from that familiar contact. I smiled. There probably really wasn't a need to tell him about how my wings could pick up his feelings. But what feelings those were: joy and contentment, and blanketing all of that, the knowledge he was safe. And loved.

I dug a little deeper into his mind, and there, where I had found loneliness and doubt and insecurity the night I and the dragon mother had rescued him from that basement, right in that place in his mind, was a sense of belonging now. It was tenuous, still new and not yet fully rooted, except for where it was connected to the image of me. There, it was firm and solid. I gasped when I sensed it. It was so much, such a miracle to find this, and on Midwinter Morning, no less. He loved me entirely, purely. I was his anchor in a raging sea, an archer he would trust blindly to shoot an apple off his own head.

Like I had from the loneliness all those weeks ago, I pulled away from this now and bent to kiss the top of his head. After so long, he was mine, finally, and he'd be that way until the end of time, or until either of us ended.

Which was why it was so painful that I would eventually have to wake him and drag him back to Copsewyck Police Station so he could give his sober-minded statement about last night.

A low, involuntary growl escaped me from just the thought of Michael attacking my Nelly, but Michael had certainly gotten a fair return on his lust for vengeance, and Nelly, well. Nelly had shown some of his true power. It served that fucking angel right, and I hoped he'd spend the rest of his mortal life with chronic diarrhea or something equally unpleasant. Hair loss, maybe.

I checked myself and stopped growling when Nelly tensed under my wings and a tendril of fear rose inside him.

"Shh, my love. I'm here, and all is well. Sleep," I whispered, but a part of him heard.

I glanced out the window. Snowflakes were obscuring the milky morning sky. I could give him five more minutes. His relaxed exhale ran over my feathers. I could give him another hour.

IT WAS ALMOST noon by the time I went about slowly waking my necromancer with a few soft kisses. Since he hadn't been tossed into a vat of coffee yet, soft kisses hardly did anything.

"Babe," I said. "Time to get up."

He grumbled excessively, but I hardly minded. I was still floating on the high of knowing that I had all of him, finally, that I was all his. And him grumbling and uncoordinated made it so I had an easy time coaxing him into the shower where he didn't resist at all when I washed him. I even indulged myself by shampooing his hair twice.

Nelly was being delightfully demure right up until I rummaged around in the lingerie shopping bag I still hadn't unpacked. That piqued his interest from where he was frowning at the bag I'd packed for the both of us, seeing as there weren't any black clothes in there for him. And no more regular underwear either.

"Mmm, this I think," I said as I handed him a box. The piece inside was one of the ones I'd bought several spares of, and I was looking forward to tearing the panties off him later that day.

Nelly eyed the white box with red lettering, frowning so much I was afraid he might get wrinkly from it.

"It's cold outside, Beelzebug. I'm not wearing—well, whatever is in there. And also, did you pack anything that isn't so, so…"

"Colorful?"

He lifted his lovely golden eyes to glare at me, and I turned my head so the faint winter light coming in through the high windows would make my damp hair shimmer.

"I'm still recovering from the damn candy cane costume of last night," he said.

I let out a long-suffering sigh. "You looked good as a candy cane, but I never got to lick you last night, babe. Open the box. I got it just for you." I considered. Mmm, getting him a little enraged could be risky, but I was the Devil and not scared of anything. "I had the salesperson model these, you know."

"You *what?*"

I shrugged. "I pointed out things I wanted for you, and then he put them on. So very helpful of him."

That Nelly could get this riled without even a drop of caffeine was an interesting development and information I needed to file away for later use.

"You had a fucking guy in some fucking store model fucking girly underwear for you because you wanted to see *me* in it?" He pointed out the window. "And you want to see me in it in the middle of a fucking snowstorm where things get cold?"

I smiled at him. "But, babe, you have me to keep you warm. And I would have preferred to take you to the lingerie store to model your own things, but I like doing the shopping while you work. Or lecture."

That took the wind right out of his sails, and apart from his deep blush, he deflated.

"Give me that," he said and snatched the box from my fingers.

I grinned. Yes, I had no doubt, no doubt at all I could get him to enthusiastically wear whatever I picked out for him.

"Are you fucking kidding me?" he said and lifted the thong off its bed of satin. I loved this one because the lace in the front looked a little bit like tiny flames lapping at his abdomen. And because it was red.

I reached into the duffel bag he'd been frowning at and pulled out a lovely blood red sweater with a single white snowflake on the chest.

"It will look wonderful with this."

He was fuming. I was happy. I had already won.

"Fine," he said, snatched the sweater from me, then got his blue jeans, and hurried into the bathroom to get changed.

That was a letdown, because I would have liked to watch him figure out how to best wear a thong, but it was fine. Being in a relationship meant you had to be willing to compromise after all.

I teleported us to the great room once we were both dressed. Unsurprisingly, Hades was kneeling next to the nest I'd built for Soul and her hellbrood, looking about ready to cry.

"Good morning," Persephone said and poured Nelly a large mug from a thermos. She and Trony were on the couch, guarded by Cerberus, since the both of them also had cucumber sandwiches and raspberry muffins. "Those two are a Saturnalia surprise." She pointed at the babies.

"I guess the poodle wasn't fluffy after all," Trony added.

Nelly gulped down half his mug before taking a seat on the couch next to Sephy. "She had them under the tree when we came down earlier," he said.

"Ugh. That thing has to be a breeding ground for spiders," Trony said. "Are we sure the hellish babies are okay?"

Nelly nodded. "Tiamat said they were."

I cleared my throat and sat next to Nelly. "Trony, I cut that tree down myself."

Hades got up, came over to us, and snatched a muffin before filling an armchair with his bulk. "Mate, you wanted a tiny spruce."

"I wanted a tree that would please my Nelly," I said and put a hand on his knee.

"It's a very… It's a hell of a tree," Nelly said. "And the light you magicked made it even more amazing."

I beamed. It felt so good to give him some of the things he'd never had as a child. Hades rolled his eyes. Hypocrite.

"You two are headed back into town, right?" Sephy asked after handing Nelly a sandwich and refilling his mug. Cerberus was trying to get my necromancer to feed him, but Nelly steadfastly ignored him, so I got a muffin and made sure to drop lots of crumbs while eating it.

"Lily said she wanted a statement," I said between bites.

Nelly sighed. "I'm not sure what to tell them."

"Just what you remember, pumpkin," Sephy said. "It's just so they have everything on file I'm sure."

"I still think you all were too merciful. We could have

just left him there. His dick would have turned into a popsicle and frozen off, and that would have been just punishment," Trony said, then put her cup down and stood. "But I have to head back to Brunswick for a few hours to take care of Jeremy. See you for the Midwinter Feast tonight."

She teleported away, and Nelly finished his sandwich and washed it down with the rest of his coffee.

"If we have to go, I'd like to get it over with," he said. "Can we teleport there?"

"You actually have to, lad," Hades said. "Been snowing since earlier, and the plow hasn't been here yet. Might not even get here before Christmas."

"We are officially snowed in," Sephy said and pointed out the large window to where the dragon mother's scales were barely visible under the snow. "But at least Tiamat enjoys it."

"I've never been snowed in before," Nelly said. He didn't sound like it would be such a terrible thing. Good.

I had never been snowed in either, but I knew it was important to keep warm, to share body heat. All night long.

SEPHY HAD VENTURED outside to the kitchen garden where she'd cut down some of the monster rhubarb for us to bring to the station so we could hand it off to the constables, and once we'd gotten dressed for the weather in the mudroom and I'd made sure Nelly's scarf was snug around his neck, I took him into my arms and pulled him close.

"No magic, babe."

"Yeah, yeah," he said, but then buried his face in my chest, the paper bag with the rhubarb held at his side. "By the way, if I end up with hypothermia of the butt because I'm not wearing proper underwear, it'll be your fault if that puts my butt out of commission until the new year. Just saying."

I stopped before I'd gathered enough magic to teleport us away and tilted his chin up with a finger instead. Oh, he knew he was being cheeky, and from his blush, he knew what it did to me too. By rights, I should be bending him over one of the wooden chairs behind us so I could give him a quick fuck, but we had places to be and rhubarb to dispense.

"I'll guard your butt as if it were my own. Which it technically is, isn't it."

For emphasis, I palmed his butt cheek and kissed him when he gasped, then went right into the teleport.

"I'll say, you'll give us all a deadly fright," Constable Lily said when we appeared at the station. Right in front of her desk.

Winston moaned a little—he didn't sound scared—and I relinquished Nelly's lips to see the older constable's jaw dropped, lip resting on the tip of his unicorn pen. The pen was shaped like a unicorn, and he was, suggestively, licking that horn. His delight at seeing a strong man like myself kissing Nelly like that was easy enough to read.

"Thank you. And sorry. So sorry," Nelly said. Mmm. Had he just thanked me for kissing him or for promising to guard his butt?

"I told you I would deliver my boyfriend so he could give you his account of events," I said and let Nelly go. "Here he is."

"And I brought rhubarb from Sephy. For additional

Christmas baking," Nelly said and put the bag on Lily's desk.

The ginger-haired constable brightened. "Lovely! There's more than baking you can do with this. My mum makes it into jelly, and rhubarb chutney is also quite good."

"So good," Winston said, and from another quick examination of his emotions, he was still enthralled and imagining the kiss between me and Nelly going on.

"Winston, get them some coffee, will you? And a few biscuits," Lily said and waved us forward to take the chairs in front of her desk.

Winston clearly had seniority in their team, but it was refreshing to see a man who didn't feel the need to insist upon having the last word. I was really looking forward to playing bridge with Winston and his partner in the new year, although I wasn't sure Nelly had been sober enough last night to realize I'd set that up.

But he'd enjoy being social. Eventually.

Winston cleared his throat and headed to the break room while Lily did things on her computer. If Scotland was anything like Brunswick, she was opening a new report in the file she'd already started last night after Michael had so rudely interrupted our wassailing.

Lily had at first complained that we had put him in the big burlap sack Trony had used for the presents, but Trony had explained that deranged humans could be dangerous, and that Hades and I (totally whipped and helpless to the every whim of our humans, and thus rendered incapable of simple murder) were not in a state to defend Sephy and Nelly in any other way. I had considered arguing, but Trony washed my socks and made my Nelly's coffee. I was the Devil, and I knew never to upset the angel working for me.

"All right. Tell me about last night, Nelly," Lily said.

Nelly shrugged. "Not much to tell." He bit his lip. "Michael attacked us and he used yetis as a distraction." Lily wrote that down without the slightest hesitation. Last night, when Trony and Sephy had told her everything, she'd needed a good pour of mead afterward, but today she seemed to have come to terms with those events. "Then he attacked. Me specifically. And I did some sort of magic."

Lily stopped. "Necromancy? You made him all human and not quite right with necromancy?"

Nelly shrugged. "You heard Hades was teaching me magic. It's…possible I might have an immortal in my ancestry."

"Hmm," Lily uttered, the keyboard clacking. "And once he was human, what did you do to him then? To make him like he is now?"

Nelly's eyebrows went up. "Nothing. I passed out after whatever I did was done, and by the time the spell had rendered him human, I was still passed out. The first I heard about it—about him being human now—was last night when you all made me drink mead."

"Excuse me, Lily, but what are you saying exactly? Michael is unsavory still, but we did nothing to make him that way. I assure you, he has always been that way." It was an understatement. Certainly, there were angels even less savory than Michael. Still, he was the kind of stinky refuse you never wanted to step into when walking down a road, but he'd always been like that.

Lily shrugged. "We had to have him taken to hospital. For a psychiatric evaluation. Was screaming and banging his head against the wall, a possible danger to himself and others, that sort of thing."

I smiled. "At last, consequences." And maybe Sephy had been right when she'd said Michael deserved that. Maybe consequences were the better punishment, although watching Michael's dick freeze off would have been prime entertainment, I was very much in agreement with Trony on that point.

"He's…gone?" Nelly asked, relief lapping at his voice.

"Well, he's in hospital," Lily said.

Nelly looked happy enough about that.

Footsteps made me turn.

"Here you go, lads," Winston said and put a tray down in front of us. The station had homemade gingerbread people, and some even had the same rainbow sprinkles Nelly and Sephy had put on the ones they had made, and unless I was mistaken, we were being treated to hot chocolate mocha with whipped cream and shaved chocolate on top. It looked very delicious.

"We don't get that in Brunswick," Nelly mumbled. He was right too.

"You need to try these. Winston says it's a secret recipe, and he only makes them around Christmas," Lily said and went for a mug.

I handed one to Nelly before taking my own.

"Traditions are important," Winston said and lifted the last mug. "Cheers."

The cheers went around our little group, and I had to say, if these lovely crime solvers ever wanted to ask my necromancer for help again, they would be welcome to him. In the strictest professional manner between the hours of nine and five.

"So can we close this case then?" Winston asked his

colleague.

"I don't see what else needs doing," Lily said. "The relevant point is that we are only responsible for any crime—potential crime—since he became human, and as we discussed, the mode of transportation was to keep both you and him safe."

"Burlap sacks are good for that," I said.

Nelly snorted. "Sure. That's why Krampus carries kids in one."

I grinned at him. "Exactly."

Lily bit the head of a gingerbread person. "We ain't putting that in the file."

"Really, if you're looking at it, you saved a naked man from freezing to death in the snow. Maybe you should get a—Lily, we still do them certificates?" Winston asked.

"Oh, the ones the mayor signs? You know, I think we do."

"Uhm, guys, we really don't want—" Nelly started.

"Oh, but we absolutely do," I said and put a hand on his leg, close to his crotch. "I want to frame it. Can it say I saved Michael's minuscule manhood from freezing off?"

"We didn't take measurements," Winston said, and Lily tsked at him.

"We cannot put the word 'manhood' on a certificate and have the mayor sign it," Lily said.

I shrugged. "I'm fine with you printing and signing it, Lily. Or the both of you, in fact."

"Aye," Winston said and turned to his own computer. "We can even stamp it, if you want."

"This is not how giving a statement normally goes," Nelly said and licked cream off his lip. Mmm. Lickable necromancer.

Before we could further discuss the certificate of

heroic dick rescue, Lily's desk phone rang.

"Copsewyck Police, this is Constable Doors speaking. Aye, I see. They what now? Yes, we know where that is, but those birds are fast and vicious. Aye, we'll help. Five minutes."

"Anything urgent?" Nelly asked and put his empty mug down. If it had caffeine, my necromancer was a bottomless hole for it.

"Three Christmas geese escaped when Warren McCormack got them out of his lorry to carry them into the butcher's, and now they cannot find them."

"Oh, well," Winston said and finished his own mocha before wiping his beard clean on a napkin. "Can't let them get frostbite when they should be going into the oven."

"You're…going out to hunt escaped Christmas geese?" Nelly asked, and I heard it in his voice: he did not like the idea of that. My Nelly loved animals, and any kind of butchery made him queasy. I knew that all too well from all the human butchery scenes I'd accompanied him to for his work.

"Small town," Lily said and pulled on her parka and neon vest before topping her outfit off with her constable hat. "Sometimes we handle small crime, but we are not above community service. It's the murder that we don't really get here."

"Indeed," Winston said as he got dressed for the outdoors as well.

Nelly pulled on the sleeve of my winter jacket, a nice one I wore to please Trony since I didn't much mind the cold.

"Those poor geese," he said quietly and looked at me with big, pleading eyes.

Uh-oh. I was in trouble. Unless I was mistaken, I

was about to be roped into civil disobedience. I was the Devil, and my disobedience was rarely civil. But I did not want to lose either mine or Nelly's Christmas mocha privileges. If the constables wanted to get the geese to the butcher and my Nelly wanted the opposite, it put me in an awkward position.

"Bah, they'll lose their heads one way or the other. We'll just have to see about them not freezing first," Winston said. "You don't worry about it, Nelly. Go enjoy the snow and a good fire to keep you warm."

"Right. You two are free to return to your Christmas preparations. We'll let Minnie know so she doesn't have a heart attack in case you walk out the front door, but feel free to finish your drinks first. And take some biscuits if you want," Lily said.

"Thank you," I said.

Once the constables had left, I turned to my necromancer, but I didn't have to say anything.

"We cannot let them catch those geese," Nelly said. "We cannot let them slaughter them. Not so close to the holidays. It wouldn't be right."

Oh, yes. He was going to make me save waterfowl from the butcher's block. I was an age-old being of immeasurable magical power and prowess, and my boyfriend was going to send me out into the snow to save *geese*. And with those bright, hopeful eyes looking at me, there was no way I would be able to deny him. But for the mocha privileges if nothing else, I had to try to make him see reason.

"Babe, we would be breaking the law. And besides, they have been bred for this."

If I'd had my wings on him, I might have realized that was the wrong thing to say. Since I hadn't, I only saw it when his face set into a harsh landscape of hurt.

"I was supposedly bred to be used," he mumbled. "The minotaur told Michael he could use me."

Anger rose, because prior to last night—prior to what Michael himself had said—Nelly hadn't told me any of this. I wanted Minos dead badly, but I couldn't do that. I couldn't do that to Nelly—make myself into his father's murderer.

And so instead, rather than trying to extract a deal in exchange for my help, I cupped my sweet necromancer's chin and said, "Of course I'll help you save the geese."

What had become of me? If anyone found out about this, my reputation would be ruined…and it would have been worth it, because Nelly was smiling up at me and looking so fucking fuckable that my cock filled instantly.

It was something I'd just have to ignore on my quest to rescue these overgrown chickens with an attitude problem.

CHAPTER THREE
LIONEL

It had to be the aftereffects of the mead or Soul's babies. Maybe it was even the realization that I usually only worked with those who were already dead with no chance at saving them at all, but I couldn't just let those geese get slaughtered.

Lucifer beamed at the older desk officer, Minnie, as we walked out like normal people and charmingly inquired where the butcher shop was. Minnie pushed her glasses back up on her nose and explained, although her accent was so thick, I couldn't follow.

Lucifer seemed fine though. Either that, or he was pretending. After a lengthy explanation of the route, we said our goodbyes to Minnie and made for the exit.

A cold wind blew in a heaping of snowflakes when I opened the door. Even under all the snow, the town and town square with its fountain looked charmingly beautiful with all the decorations: wreaths and red ribbons hung on the eaves of store fronts and buildings, plastic Santas and star-shaped lights with the odd reindeer and sleigh thrown in shimmered brightly while the day was overcast, and through the store windows, I could see even more elaborate displays that had been set up inside.

The shop owners had been doing a great job of keeping the sidewalks clear, and the shoe shop owner—Lucifer had paraded me around in front of her too not too long ago when we'd gotten the dragon mother her present—was clearing the area in front of her shop as I watched. She spotted us and gave an enthusiastic wave. Lucifer returned it with the same enthusiasm.

"Ready?" Lucifer asked when he was back to being focused all on me. He took the opportunity to fuss with my scarf and cap, because him fussing with my underwear wasn't bad enough. Ugh. Okay, and maybe it was also nice to know he made sure I wasn't cold, maybe that too.

"Yes. Where are we going? I had trouble understanding Minnie."

He chuckled. "Takes your ears a while to get used to it. We'll take the backstreets." He put an arm around my shoulders and drew me along. "I don't think we should be seen. Saving geese."

"I'm on vacation. I can do whatever the fuck I want when I'm on vacation," I said, then wondered whether he'd think this was idiotic, the kind of thing not worthy of his attention. It would have been easy to give up and ask him to take me home, but wasn't trust something that took continued effort? And I…I liked that he was here and willing to do this with me.

He sighed. "If only you wanted to kneel in front of me more, with your pretty ass all ready for me and your cock hard and leaking. But I meant we don't want to be seen sidestepping the law by Winston and Lily."

My cheeks heated. Because the idea of being on my knees for him… It was odd to want to do things like that for him knowing he'd like it. It made me feel good though. To think about it. To know if I asked him for anything, he'd do it, give it. I'd just never had that ever before.

And I was glad he was aware that we couldn't be seen technically stealing geese that weren't ours. "Right. That would be awkward. If they saw us."

"Exactly."

We turned left and had to pick up our feet, because in the small alleys between houses, the snow had gathered in deep drifts. But that all made me giddy, because Copsewyck was an ancient little town, and the buildings were old, stone or timber frame, and I felt like I'd been whisked backward through time.

For a moment as we walked side by side, I imagined I was a prince—no, not a prince, I was just an orphan living on the streets, and he was the prince. He'd found me, had wrapped me in a warm coat, and was now taking me to his castle to live happily ever after. Something about the age-old houses around us, built in haphazard angles to form crisscrossing alleys, and the fresh snow burying it all, it made the fantasy seem that much sweeter. And the geese we were about to save, maybe they were my enchanted brothers, cursed by an evil mage to remain like that until they found true love.

"Do you think they are okay?" I asked Lucifer when he walked ahead of me through another snow dune so as to make a path I could easily follow.

He looked left and right when the alley spilled us out onto a slightly larger road. Trees had been planted here, but their branches were barren and black under the snow and ice, though around those branches, the townsfolk had draped fairy lights that shimmered on as I watched.

"Who? The geese? Are you worried about the geese?"

"Well, yeah? It's cold. And snowy. Imagine them falling into high snow like that. They might suffocate."

The road here was residential and all timber framed with the dates of when the houses had been erected carved into the wood. Dragons and boars also featured as decorative elements. The snow was quickly covering everything, but I was pretty sure the road was cobblestones underneath all the white, and I wouldn't mind some sightseeing once spring came. Copsewyck really was a nice place.

"The one thing I will say about geese—apart from their irrationally aggressive streak—is that they aren't dumb. They wouldn't hop into the snow, babe," Lucifer said. Then he came to an abrupt halt, cursed in a consonant-heavy language, and bodily tossed me into a snow dune that lived in a narrow gap between two houses I wouldn't even call an alley.

I landed on my ass. What the fuck? Before I could complain or struggle back to my feet, he was on top of me.

"What—"

"Guarding your sensitive butt, babe," the Devil purred and squeezed the body part in question.

"What I meant was, why am I on my ass in the snow?"

"Mmm. Lily was just coming around the corner. She'd have seen us."

Just as he said it, I heard her. "Come out, come out, little geese," she said. "Too cold to be quacking about."

"Fuck. She's going to see us when she walks past here, and I'm not using fucking in the snow as an excuse," I said, because boundaries like that were important in a relationship.

Lucifer chuckled and looked at me as if he wanted

to say, *Oh, canary, nothing like fucking in the snow to steam up your life.*

"Shame. I could've made sure your butt isn't frostbitten."

I felt his magic then. I realized it felt so very familiar now, just like when we teleported or even when he did his silly overly slippery sex magic.

The snow obeyed his spell and covered us, a perfect blanket of white that bathed us in milky, snowy light.

"Wow," I said. It was easy to forget he could do actual kinetic spells when he mostly used his magic for different things. Such as lubing me up like a car in a car wash.

"Please, even human magic users could do this," he said, voice hardly lowered.

"Shh!"

"Silence ward, babe."

"Oh. Right. And I think this is more mage-level stuff. I mean, it's god-level stuff. But you know. In terms of human magic."

"Mmm. Please don't talk about me in terms of human magic. I still cannot believe your magic school failed to initiate you into the very basics of magic use for sex. Such a disgrace, so much knowledge lost over the years, and all the nice human magic users the poorer for it."

For emphasis, he did something. It was just a touch of magic reaching inside me and gone almost as soon as I'd felt it, but my hole still clenched—very annoying with the thong—and I gasped. And seriously, who had even dreamed up thongs? Those things had no practical value whatsoever, and they were uncomfortable and intrusive to wear.

"S-stop that!"

He chuckled and kissed the side of my mouth. "Stop

what? I'm not doing anything." And the ass squeezed my butt again.

"Stop it!" I said, then froze because there was a shadow above us.

"Geese, where are you?" Lily called out.

I held my breath. She wouldn't poke our snow dune, would she? If she did… I couldn't tell her we were trying to save the geese. Fuck. We'd have to lie. And say it was kinky fucking in the snow after all.

But the shadow passed, as did Lily's voice. I let out the breath I'd been holding and relaxed.

"Babe, please tell me you weren't worried she might see us," Lucifer said.

"You never know. Is she gone? We need to find those geese before they freeze."

"Fine," Lucifer said, sighing. "Up you get."

Before I knew what was what, the snow blanket disintegrated, and I was being deadlifted off the snow and bridal carried back to the small street where I was reluctantly put on my feet and the remaining snow brushed off my coat. Lucifer made sure my cap and scarf where in place. Ridiculous, but again, nice, because his fingers left trails of warmth against my skin.

"That was close," I said.

"It wasn't. My magic is perfect," Lucifer grumbled.

Uh-oh. Alpha god ego alert. I counted myself very lucky that Persephone had taught me all about that, and so I cleared my throat. I could do this. I was a half-human necromantic police consultant on vacation, and I could reassure the overpowered alpha god I loved that he was the best.

"I know that. It's just that I'm not used to seeing magic come this easily to anyone other than mages, and since I never dated a mage"—He growled.—"something I have zero interest in ever doing and wouldn't have wanted to experience, I'm pleasantly surprised. I'm sorry I suck at expressing that."

"You just felt my magic earlier today, and I have always delivered us to the intended place when I teleported us, babe."

Okay. So he was still upset, but he was also clearly goal oriented and leading me through the erratically winding tiny streets of the town.

"Yeah, you have. But you mostly just walk into a place and know everyone's names and get things done without magic. It makes me forget how powerful you are, but when I see it—"

Lucifer spun and—very carefully—slammed me into a house wall. "Babe, you forget how powerful I am?" he asked, sounding like the cat asking the canary whether he'd missed those lovely teeth beyond the whiskers. Clearly I had said the wrong thing to soothe my alpha god's ego, and I wasn't sure what Persephone would do.

"Uhm…"

He started grinning. "Tell me the truth, babe."

"Uhm, your hair looks very soft, and I love the snowflakes in it." I reached up and brushed along a strand. The snowflakes there stuck to my gloves, and a few tumbled away. The Devil started making his Devil noises.

"Nelly. Do you want me to get your cock cage right now? And put it on you right here in this alley?"

My jaw dropped, and I shook my head. Oh, if only my boyfriend were a god of empty threats.

"Good. Then tell me. Do you forget how powerful I am?"

I cleared my throat. "Well, it's not like I think you are some human, you know. But…you are just Lucy to me, my Lucy, and not some all-powerful deity who seduces people and never lies and is incredibly good at sex."

My heart rate picked up, because telling him stuff like this was still so new. And scary. A month ago, I'd have weaseled my way out of this with something incredibly sarcastic. And I'd likely have found my cock caged as a result. This was scarier, a million times scarier.

"Look at me," my Devil commanded. "Good. I have never been called anything that was truer. I am your Lucy." He put his palm right under my throat where beneath the layers of fabric and warm against my skin I wore the choker with his image under resin. "But you should also know my power in your blood, in your every cell. You will, my love, before the sun rises again after this longest night."

My mouth was watering, and my cock was stirring, both very inappropriate reactions, and by that smile, the Devil *knew,* he knew what his sex talk was doing to me. The things I was willing to do in order to allow his ego to rub one out.

"Does…your power help us find these geese?"

"Oh, babe. Now you are just asking to be edged all night."

CHAPTER FOUR

LUCIFER

Firstly, I wanted to be in bed, my cock buried in Nelly's ass so there was zero chance of hypothermia of the butt. Secondly, geese did not deserve my necromancer's tenacity, because no one liked them, no one. They were fucking assholes who reveled in attacking people for no good reason, except that one time in Rome, and even then, it might have been a lucky accident.

Either way, the sooner we found the fowl, the sooner I could get back to showing my necromancer how very powerful my magic was. What he'd really been saying—and I didn't think he was aware of this, like was typical for him—was that he no longer thought of immortals as strange, otherworldly creatures, the boogeymen and -women the reports he'd read during his studies likely made us out to be. And that was a good thing, because his magic, his demigod magic, made him more like me than any other human mage. He just wasn't willing to admit that to himself yet, but what he'd done to Michael proved it.

With my cock hard and straining, it took all my divine effort to focus on the task at hand. We squeezed past two trash cans and came out right next to the old town wall when, finally, I spotted something.

"Hah." I squatted to pick the white feather from the snow. There were waddling footprints here as well, and I pointed at them. "They passed through here."

"I get the feather, but what am I looking at?" Nelly asked, looking over my shoulder.

Well, he was a necromancer, and not a hunter, so I didn't expect him to know anything related to hunting.

"Goose footprints," I said and pointed before standing back up and following them.

"How can you even tell?"

They went along the old wall until we came to an archway set into it. From there a staircase led down to the street level about a story or so below us. The stairs were cordoned off and had an ice warning sign.

"I do know how to hunt things, babe," I said and lifted the sign before taking a quick step back into Nelly.

"What?"

"Neon vest and bowler hat. That's Winston down there." I pushed Nelly back and to the side so the wall hid us. Damn those constables, but they took public service seriously.

Nelly leaned around me to peek through the archway. "Fuck. What if he finds them first?"

Well, I couldn't let that happen, could I? I had to impress my necromancer, and if saving those fucking geese was the way to do it, then so be it.

"He won't, babe." I pulled him off his feet and into my arms, and his grunting complaint was halfhearted at best. "Hold on to me." And with that, I brought my wings out and took off.

"Oh, we're flying!" he said. Mmm. I had a feeling he

would like Sephy's Saturnalia present quite a bit.

"That's what wings are for," I said and ignored that pang of…something. He absolutely didn't need to know that my wings were for something else as well. There was no need.

"There's Winston. Won't he be able to see us?" he asked, shielding his eyes with a hand. It was still snowing heavily, and demigod or not, if you weren't made for flight, weather in your eyes put a dampener on the experience.

"Not in this weather, and not with my magic making sure he won't."

The real issue was that *I* couldn't see from up there either, especially not geese trails that were being covered as we were flying.

I scanned the area as best as I could and landed in the street next to a dry cleaner's and a small grocery store. I had a hunch, because geese really were not stupid, just mean motherfuckers. If I was right, we'd still have to hurry because Winston was coming around the building from the other side.

"Wow, it was cold up there," Nelly said when I put him back on his feet. "Did you spot them? The geese?"

I shook my head. "No, but I do have an idea. Come on, we have to hurry."

He nodded and actually hooked his arm under mine. I grinned, and after three steps, I heard a frustrated quack, and my grin broadened.

We walked around the building—around the grocery store next to the dry cleaner's—and right there, behind another trash can, the A/C exhaust spilled out warm air, a bubble in which the three feathery fiends were sheltering.

Nelly let out a relieved sigh when he saw them and went straight for them, completely abandoning me.

"Babe, careful, don't touch them. They bite."

"It's fine," my necromancer said and didn't even stop. And the fucking geese, their beady eyes much too intelligent for creatures that looked like ducks with stretchy necks, took one look at Nelly, quacked once each in greeting, and waddled into his open arms without a touch of aggression or fear.

Okay, I knew Nelly was good with animals, but this was uncanny.

I was about to say as much, but of course in that exact moment, I spotted the neon vest across from the gap between buildings, and so I dove for Nelly and the gaggle.

The geese immediately went berserk, quacking and squawking like the beasts they were. I drew a silencing ward and spelled the snow around us to cover us, and Nelly hooked his arms around the three geese necks I'd have loved to snap, containing them.

"Oh, fuck you," I said to the one closest to me. It was eyeing me and clicking its beak. If given the chance, that one would go for my balls, I just knew it.

"Shh, you're fine now. Lucy and I are going to help you," Nelly said.

"Yes, we are the knights in these geese's fairy tale life," I said.

Nelly turned around and grinned at me. "I guess we are," he said, and damn. He was happy. He was glad we'd found the geese first and saved their feathery skins. My cock gave a needy twitch that couldn't go anywhere, not right now, but soon.

"Can you teleport us? Uhm, where do geese live?" Nelly said and petted one of them. It seemed to calm the goose.

"Someplace warm." Maybe an active volcano or a nice, cozy barbecue. I sighed. These geese had to be kept safe though, no matter that one goose was still glaring at me with murder in their eyes. "You know what? I think we can bring them to the zoo."

He looked at me, and when the dark shadow of Winston passed over us, he froze, clutched the geese tighter to him, and they shut up as if they could sense his unease.

"He can't hear anything," I said.

On the other side of the snow cover, a police radio clicked to live.

"Have you found them yet?" Lily asked, her voice distorted and metallic over the connection.

"Nah. I thought I heard something, but there's nothing here."

"Shite. Let's give it another twenty minutes, and then we give up. I can barely feel my toes anymore."

"Aye, sounds good. I'll make us a cuppa once we get back to the station. Twenty more minutes."

The radio clicked off, and Winston passed.

"Phew. You were saying about the zoo? Brunswick Zoo?" Nelly asked.

"Yes, babe. You could visit them there."

Nelly's fingers caressed the geese's feathers, and jealousy burned hot in me. He was supposed to love *my* feathers the most. Fucking fowl interlopers.

"Would you like that? To live in a zoo? You'd be safe there. Doesn't that sound good? No one would want to eat you for dinner, and there are no butchers in a zoo." He turned but luckily kept the geese contained. "Let's do that."

"Right." I wrapped an arm around his middle from

behind. The geese were looking at me over his shoulders, clearly aiming to bite my eyeballs. "No magic, babe."

I teleported us quickly. I needed the fucking geese away from my boyfriend, and then I needed to remind him he was supposed to give *me* most of his attention.

"Oh, I've never actually been here," Nelly said when we arrived inside the zoo, which was illuminated by lanterns set along its winding paths. The enclosures themselves were still dark.

Brunswick greeted us with a salty night breeze, because with the time difference, darkness here had not yet lifted. It had to be the earlier hours of the morning. It was pretty cold here too although it wasn't snowing at the moment.

When Nelly dropped his arms and stood, the geese remained close to him as if they wanted to claim him. Oh, those fuckers. It was bad enough that Marc Deacon thought he had a chance with Nelly. Now there were these things too, and while Marc, objectively, had nothing Nelly liked, the geese had *feathers*. And Nelly loved a nice set of wings and how soft feathers felt when he touched them.

"You should have told me you've never been to the zoo," I said. "I'd have happily taken you."

Nelly gave me a shy smile, and one of the geese noticed he was paying me attention, so it positioned itself between us and quacked, the little fucker.

"Hello? Excuse me, but we closed hours ago," said a human in zookeeper uniform, though she was wearing a nice warm jacket and fur lined boots. As she approached, I saw her red, baggy eyes. She looked like she'd been up all night.

"We're sorry," Nelly said and pointed at his three new

friends. "Do you have a place for them?"

The zookeeper came closer, but if she had a nametag, it was obscured by her jacket. She stared wide-eyed but was surprisingly not freaked out by two strangers and three fowl appearing in this closed area. Who knew? Maybe this happened often.

"Obviously, we'd adopt them to ensure they have a wonderful rest of their lives," I said through gritted teeth. I would prefer the rest of their lives be short, but I could not say that. Not when I saw Nelly looking up at me like he was doing now. "I'll write you a check, Miss?"

"Amanda Kouri. Is this some sort of animal rescue?"

Nelly crossed his arms. "Nope. Not at all. We found them. Just walking around. In fact, I'm a consultant with Brunswick PD. A necromantic consultant, and he's my boyfriend and also an immortal, which is how we got in here. We just didn't want them to catch cold out in the snow, you know?" One of the geese quacked as if it agreed with all of that.

I smiled my warmest smile at Amanda while I marveled at how easily lying came to my necromancer.

Amanda massaged the bridge of her nose. "Okay, fine, but just because I'm not in a mood to call animal rescue. Follow me."

"Thanks, thank you so much," Nelly said.

"Yes, thank you for taking them off our hands," I added.

"Yeah, whatever. Better be the kind of check you'd write for some holiday fundraiser though."

Which I took as my cue to write just such a check. While the geese obediently walked along with Nelly, I pulled out my checkbook and pen. I handed the check to Amanda as we walked past the sleeping lions and tigers, and she gasped.

"Is that not enough?" I asked.

"W-what? No, no, this is very generous."

Nelly, surrounded by his geese, frowned at me, but he didn't say anything.

After a nice little walk, we got to the domesticated animals, and Amanda unlocked what was basically a large farm building.

She switched on a light, and inside it smelled like animal, not unlike the horse stables back in Scotland.

"We have the guinea pigs and rabbits in here," Amanda said and walked us past an enclosure of large rabbits, who blinked at us sleepily. "I need to put your geese in quarantine." She opened a sliding door next to the rabbits. "Get them in there."

Nelly nodded, and fuck. By the time he had hugged and said goodbye to each of the geese, he was looking about ready to cry.

"You'll be fine here, I promise," he said and closed the door. The three geese never took their eyes off of him.

"Awesome. You can stay with them. I'll just fill out your names and give you a receipt," Amanda said, and I followed her into a small office to take care of the paperwork.

AMANDA KOURI HAD warmed up considerably after she'd watched my sweet necromancer stare at the geese through the bars of their quarantine home and after I'd shown interest in all the photos of animals and keepers in the small, cluttered office.

She'd returned to watching over a heavily pregnant anteater, and so Nelly and I were left to wander through the zoo by ourselves.

"That felt good," he said after a little while, leaning into my side.

I had plans to make everything feel even better.

"I do hope Winston and Lily had a chance to warm up by now," I said and inhaled his scent. The sharpness of his demigod magic had almost vanished again, almost, but not quite.

"Yeah. It is pretty cold, isn't it? But look at all those stars."

I stopped and pulled him into my arms so we could both look up. "Very pretty," I said, looking at the three stars forming Orion's belt before letting my gaze drop to Nelly's eyes. "Very pretty indeed."

His cheeks heated, and his arms tightened around me.

"Stop flattering me," he said. "You really don't have to."

"Mmm. No flattery, babe. Just the truth. But I can see you are cold, and I should warm you up. Come."

I released him from my arms but took his hand and turned right at the fork in the path ahead. There was a single lantern in front of the building I wanted to get into.

"The herpetarium? We can't go in there. It's closed."

"Babe, you know the wonderful thing about being a divine creature?" I put my hand on the door and cast a simple spell. "All you need is a little bit of magic, and all doors are open to you."

"But we can't—"

"Oh, we can," I said and pulled him across the

threshold.

Inside it was warmer, noticeably so, and in the terrariums, heat lamps were on so that the entire place was not quite dark. What light there was made it look magical, enchanted, even though it was just electricity and glass.

"I think we are trespassing."

"Well, babe, we are already guilty of fowl theft, so this is hardly worse." There was a lizard lounging on a log to our left, but on the right, there was a python, an albino, red eyes looking black in the light. I spun Nelly around, unfolded my wings and wrapped them around him, then pushed him up against the python's glass. "In fact, I think we need to add public indecency to our list of felonies."

"What?" he said, voice small and breathy, pupils wide with the lacking light.

"I need to make sure nothing's frozen down here." I reached to palm his ass cheeks and massaged them. "I need to make sure you don't feel neglected. And I need to make sure we're celebrating this almost longest night as we should."

"But it's not—it's not technically even night yet. In Scotland."

"We're not in Scotland right now," I said, and then I kissed him.

He yielded easily, opened up to me and gasped for air between giving me all the access I wanted.

"Unbutton your coat for me," I told him, and he barely hesitated before working it open.

I loved having him in my wings like this, loved feeling him under my long feathers and cradling his head in the arch of my wings. It gave me only some of his emotions because he was wearing too many clothes, but the glimpses were enough.

His coat falling open reminded him of his other coat, the black one I'd made him put on over the lingerie that first time.

I smiled against his temple. "I like that you're wearing your new underwear for me, babe. Especially with a coat." I pulled his sweater up and ran a finger along the waistband of his jeans. "These are in the way though."

"N-not here," he said when I undid the button of his jeans and pulled the zipper down.

"Only the snake is watching, and it doesn't care." I shoved his jeans down just as far as was necessary. His own cock was hard, the thong barely containing it. I wasn't sure whether I should let him come though, or whether I should make him wait a little longer, make him a little desperate.

Then again, he'd be doubly pliable if I let him come, and that would be nice for the Midwinter Feast. Mmm. On the other hand, our short trip here gave me an idea.

I bent down to take his mouth again and carefully worked my magic on him. He gasped and shivered, more so when I bit and sucked his bottom lip. I made it last, slowly cleaned and slicked him.

"Too much," he mumbled.

"It's not." I let my right hand wander and dipped a finger into his warm heat. The thong was perfect for getting where I wanted with ease. "See?" I said when he clenched briefly and then relaxed for me. "Slides right in."

The angle was not ideal to stretch and touch him like I wanted, but after earlier this morning, he wouldn't need that much preparation, and I certainly wasn't going to move too much or let him move too much.

"W-we can't do this in here. What if the zookeeper comes back in?"

"I have you in my wings, my love. There is nothing to see." I slipped my middle finger inside him as well and scissored both fingers open. I wanted him, badly.

"But, Lucy—"

"She might hear you, of course, but she won't be able to see this lovely red lace." I cupped his cock with my other hand, just briefly. Yes, he was enjoying this, but I had decided. He'd not come right now, and we'd make a quick stop back home before we returned to Scotland.

After all, the greatest benefit of a thong was that it really wasn't in the way when you were taking your sweet necromancer in a darkened reptile exhibit.

I spun Nelly around. "Lean on my wings, babe. Yes, that's it. Come on, push out your ass, you know what I want."

"Lucy…" he said, sounding utterly shy, even as he did what I wanted, presenting. Offering himself.

"That's right." I unzipped my jacket and pants, and my cock throbbed with the need to feel him. "Let's see if you are slick enough." I pulled his thong aside, just enough so I could push past his ring with the head of my cock.

Nelly's hands, still in gloves, closer around my feathers, and maybe it was the dark or the gloves keeping him from feeling the feathers underneath, but for once, he didn't relax immediately, didn't get the pang of fear about destroying my feathers or leaving a mark on them. He just kept going, and so did I.

I'd never believed that sex with someone you loved from the bottom of your heart was different from sex with just anyone, but it was. That moment when he'd taken all of me into him, when he shivered and turned his head to blink his golden eyes at me, even though he would only be able to see outlines, it was a moment that turned into a feeling, and that feeling made my whole body and spirit ring with elation.

I gentled my hold on his hips, reaching forward so his cock nestled on my palm even as my fingertips explored lower, to his taint. My other hand went up to his chest, adding even more support. Each touch, each reaction to my touch, brought familiarity and pleasure, trust on Nelly's part because he relaxed, or relaxed as much as he could with my cock up his tight ass. I'd never felt this kind of easy joy with another, and now that I had him, I never wanted to.

I started moving, slowly at first, and Nelly arched his back, mouth seeking my own. I didn't make him wait long for the kiss he craved, wordlessly giving it to him even as I took what I wanted.

The sex itself was not the elaborate kind that took a lot of time and usually ended on a very rewarding note, but I didn't need it to be.

"Hnn, Lucy," Nelly moaned between thrusts and sloppy kisses, body tense and hot around me.

"Just a little longer, I'm almost there."

I fucked into him with the single-minded goal of cumming, and while I felt him, his cock leaking into the lace against my palm, I never gave him more stimulation, never enough, not quite, not yet, just enough to drive him wild.

When it came, my release hit me hard and fast, and the satisfaction of filling him with everything I had to give was just as good now as it had been the first time I'd done it, as it had been every day after.

"Well done," I said, giving another lazy thrust into his now even slicker channel.

He whimpered. "More, please."

"No," I said. "No magic, babe."

I teleported without pulling out of him right into our room in our house in Brunswick. The familiarity of my own wards was nice, and so was the smell of home.

"W-where are we?" Nelly asked, sounding even shyer now that he had even less light to see by, just my wings and the city's distant brightness coming in through the windows.

"Home," I said and pulled out of him before guiding him to our bed and putting him on it, face first.

"Hey! What are you—"

"Don't move. Stay just like you are."

"With my ass out and my boots still on? Trony is going to kill me. Can you turn on a light at least?"

I chuckled as I opened the drawer of the bedside table and found what I wanted.

"Let's keep the light off for now. I want you to feel, not see."

"I can feel your cum inside me, Beelzebug, and I—"

He gasped prettily when I slapped his naked ass and pushed the dark purple plug where my cock had just been. Oh, the idea my cum would be inside him for the rest of the night or at least until I took him again, that was a thrill totally worth Trony's anger. Because the angel would be unhappy about the floor, but I would weather her wrath.

"That's right, I want you to feel my cum inside you all through this longest night, babe." I licked the shell of his ear. "Or at least until I feel the need to put more inside you. I don't have to spell this plug, do I? You'll leave it right where I want it, won't you? Tell me you'll be good for me, my love."

I liked the darkness, because even if his face was half buried in the sheets, I could see the emotions wage their battle on it, and since he couldn't see, he didn't think of hiding those emotions. I sensed what he felt even stronger when I feathered my wingtips over his naked butt. His stubborn side wanted out, but he was still reeling from how good it felt to have opened himself up to me. I kissed him behind the ear, in that spot he liked.

"I'll be good," he said.

"You like being ready for me, don't you?"

His Adam's apple bobbed. "I do."

"Good. Turn on your back."

He obeyed flawlessly, although by now, he was properly tangled up in all the winter clothes, but that wouldn't matter for much longer.

When he was on his back, I slid off him and kneeled on the floor in front of him. It wouldn't need much to get him to spill, and I hooked my fingers under his thong and pulled it down so his cock bobbed up toward me. The lace was damp with his precum, and my mouth watered even before I took him inside.

This way, I always got more of his magic, could taste it better. There was something deeply seductive to that wine taste, something that made you want more, and the blowjob I gave him was a greedy thing, was me telling him I needed more, more than he could give.

While I worked on him, I gave my own cock a few, lazy tugs, but I wouldn't waste anything, not when I could have him again in not too long, or at least if we managed to sneak out during the Midwinter Feast.

"Lucy, I'm about to—ah!"

Yes, he tasted wonderful when he came, and I licked up every last bit of him, all of it, and feasted my eyes on the spent, slightly sweaty necromancer who smiled up at me when I stood and shook out my wings for him.

Midwinter simply was the most wonderful time of the year.

CHAPTER FIVE
LIONEL

Lucifer vanished from my line of sight and his starlight wings along with him. He was headed to the wardrobe area of his bedroom. I closed my eyes for a second and just floated on the happy hormones. When I opened them again and looked down on myself, he was stroking my balls, except, that wasn't everything he was doing.

"Hey!" But the lock of the damn custom cock cage had already clicked shut.

"Yes?"

"Seriously? Get that thing off."

He shook out his wings again, and especially in the darkness, they looked so beautiful.

"No. I like it on you."

And with that, the Devil, my boyfriend, pulled the thong back up and over the cross between chastity cage and gates of hell, which still allowed me to get hard, but not quite all the way, and not enough to actually come. It was the most frustrating sensation ever.

"Fuck you."

He chuckled as he pulled my pants back up and

closed them. "That's never how it goes. I get to fuck you, babe, always."

I rolled my eyes in the darkness, and…smiled up at the ceiling. Was I broken? No, not really. Was this fun? Yes, in the weirdest of ways. Did I want him horny all night? If it was for me, yeah. Because he was the Devil, and he'd done fowl crime with me and maybe even on my orders. He deserved a reward for that.

LUCIFER TELEPORTED US straight back to the castle's courtyard, between the entrance we used most of the time and the stables. The snowfall had not let up, but a path to the stables had been kept cleared, or as cleared as was possible.

It was still light out, and we walked through the crunching snow and waved to the dragon mother in her dragon form, who acknowledged us by standing and shaking the snow off her. The way it was coming down, and the way it had piled up around her, she'd done that in intervals, because if she didn't, she'd be snowed in like everything else. For some reason, I'd always thought that winter in Brunswick with all the cold ocean air was intense, but Scotland was something else.

We made our way to the mudroom, and while the cold was bracing, being back inside was good, not for the warmth of the place, but for the smell: home and cinnamon, a rhubarb pie in the oven, food and the holiday cookies we'd baked.

Lucifer kept a protective hand on my plugged ass when we walked into the kitchen, and my mouth fell open.

"Whoa. Did you make all this?" I asked Persephone.

She was decorating a gingerbread pie thing with real holly leaves and turned at our arrival.

"Only some of it. Hades helped, and some of this is Trony's." She indicated the plates and serving dishes. "But it's good to have you back. After last night didn't go as planned, we are doing something else for the Feast."

Lucifer clucked his tongue. "Breaking tradition? I love when you are being a rebel, Sephy."

Cerberus came around the kitchen island, the left head focused on me as it always was, but it sat and gave me puppy eyes. There was all this food, and there was always a chance I would realize no one ever fed Cerberus. He was being the perfectly sweet doggie all this time, and almost too weak to function from starvation, and his eyes implored me to take note. I ignored him.

Persephone wiped her hands on a tea towel. "We've been wanting to do this for a long time, and as a matter of fact, doing it today was Hades' idea." Sephy got two envelopes out from next to a plate with puff pastries. "We're doing a murder mystery." She handed us each an envelope. "Not your regular murder mystery, of course. Let's say this one got the Midwinter death god upgrade. There are costumes in your room, and these are your roles and goals as well as the rules of the game. The whole mystery has as many variations as players, and Hades did the magic so no one knows which version we're playing, meaning we don't know who's our murderer."

"Ooh," Lucifer said. "Trony has been wanting to do one of these too."

I snorted. "Let me guess. She couldn't figure out how to incorporate an orgy into one, and that's why you told her no."

The Devil grinned at me and squeezed my ass, which made me feel the plug in such a way that made breathing difficult. And when I reacted to the feeling, the cage made its presence known. Frustrating. Fucking frustrating was what it was to be at Lucifer's mercy.

"Exactly. But maybe we can start working on that tonight."

Persephone rolled her eyes. "Why, oh why, do big strong gods always get extra horny near the end of the year? I should give you fair warning though, there is murder in this murder mystery, and if you only rely on your cock to do the thinking, Lucy, you might get murdered."

He reached for one of the cookies we'd made, and Cerberus whined when Lucifer ate it whole. "If push comes to shove, there is always ghost sex."

Persephone gave me a level look. "As a necromancer, you better know how to handle a ghost that wants into your pants if that should happen."

Lucifer waited for my response while he ate another cookie, to Cerberus's frustration.

"You don't need necromancy. I think the best way to handle a haunting is to ignore it. Because most of the time, you imagine the ghost to be bigger than he really is."

I wasn't sure what had ridden me there, but Lucifer's nostrils flared, and he looked like he wanted to pounce and show me how big he really was, right between the salad bowls and serving dishes.

In the end, he was calm and his voice smooth like all the ropes and restraints he liked to use on me. "You might end up as the haunting, my love, which would be wonderful, because ghosts never sleep or tire. And they never wear anything under their sheets."

Persephone laughed. "Spooky. You have to wait for all of that until the game has started though, and we can only start when everyone is ready, so read the instructions and get dressed."

"Of course, Sephy," Lucifer said, but his eyes were on me. He was imagining me dressed in nothing but a sheet, I just knew he was. Gods, but that cock cage was fucking tight.

BEFORE WE WENT to our room, we stopped by to check on Soul and her two babies. They had several more fluffy blankets in their nest now, and bowls of food and water for Soul so she didn't have to move much. As it was, the hellpoodle was napping while the two babies nursed. Quincey's snake tail tongued the air before it bit into one of his sister's tails. The whole scene was pretty adorable.

We took the long way back to our room after that, and Lucifer probably enjoyed watching me walk around, because each step made me remember that I was caged and plugged for him and wearing lace to please him on top of all that.

Back in our room, there were two clothes bags on our bed.

"I might enjoy a fancy murder mystery party," Lucifer said and snagged the one with his name on its tag.

I sighed and looked at the envelope in my hand. "I had to dress up like a candy cane only yesterday and look how that ended."

Lucifer unzipped the clothes bag but looked from its contents back to me. "As I said, I didn't get to lick you at all. Such a shame."

"You just made up for that, like, ten minutes ago."

"Mmm, not even a little bit. Come here, my love."

I followed the lure of his voice straight into his arms until I was wrapped in his warmth and the scent of fire and spices.

"Nothing like yesterday will happen today, sweet," he said and cupped the back of my head before feathering a kiss on my forehead. "We'll celebrate until the sun rises again, and you won't be alone through the longest night."

A shiver ran up my spine, not because this was especially sexy, but because…I'd always been alone around this time of the year. Unless there'd been an ongoing investigation or a death that required me to come to the morgue. This though, family, celebrating with them, the constant company, it was still all new.

"Lucy?"

"Yes, babe?"

"Thanks for stealing geese with me."

He sighed. "I am willing to do crime whenever you ask me to. But maybe let's not tell people we spent the afternoon saving other people's Christmas dinner."

I grinned up at him. "I think we should tell everyone." An idea hit me. I had to try this, see whether it worked. "But you know what would make me keep quiet about the geese? If I didn't have to wear the plug and cage."

He bristled. "What does the one have to do with the other?"

I shrugged. "It's how my brain works. My tongue always gets a lot looser when my ass is plugged."

"What a ridiculous notion."

"It's not like you'll touch me if I get drunk anyway," I said, because he very much wouldn't. "Plus, this thong is filthy, and I need a change of underwear if I'm to wear a costume."

Lucifer hesitated and looked down at me thoughtfully. A rush of power went through me. Had I done that? Had I just gotten the Devil to reconsider his sexy plans for the longest night?

"The change of underwear I'll grant," he said. "And I'll release you from your plug and cage by the second course of the Feast if you entertain me well through the first course. Deal?"

I swallowed the lump in my throat. I had no idea what precisely that meant, but…I felt the cage growing tighter, and I…liked the idea of this game. What was wrong with me?

"Deal," I said, my voice barely a whisper.

Lucifer smiled down at me, and I shivered because he looked as if he wanted to eat me up or eat me out, or— was there anything else that could potentially happen? In all likelihood, I was about to find out.

"Good. We should get dressed now. And get acquainted with our roles. I'll bring your change of underwear to dinner. For now, I like you in that thong. Red suits you."

I snorted. I should have learned that lesson, should have asked for a clear timeline of delivery, but Lucifer had distracted me.

"You're impossible," I said.

He palmed my ass and massaged so the plug shifted and put pressure on my prostate. I gasped.

"Am I really?"

"Unhand my ass," I said and scrambled back, snatching my clothes bag as I went. I saw something in dark velvet in his. What kind of costumes were these?

"Mmm, but, babe, I have to make sure there's no late-onset hypothermia of the butt. In your butt."

I wanted to tell him to go fuck himself, but of course that wasn't how it went, the other way around, always, so I opted for lifting my chin, holding the costume in front of me like a shield, and striding into the bathroom to get changed as best as I was able to stride, given that I was still his plaything.

"My butt is fine, and you know it," I said before closing the bathroom door behind me.

Inside the bathroom, I wondered what had just happened. Had I gotten my alpha god to do what I wanted, or had he gotten the deal he wanted? Why could I never really tell the difference?

I put the clothes bag on the counter and opened it. "What the fuck?"

Then I tore open the envelope and read the heading. "You have to be fucking kidding me."

THE COSTUME FIT perfectly, even with the damn cock cage. On the plus side, it had a cape, and I tried it with hood on and off in front of the mirror.

"Hood off. I can do this. Everyone's going to be wearing a silly costume, and this will be fun."

I turned on the water and splashed my face one last time before finally walking outside.

Lucifer was lounging in the chair by the windows and turned to me. The sun was setting, not that it made much difference with the snow still coming down. We were truly getting snowed in, which was upsetting, given that we were all snowed in with a fictional murderer.

"Hello there," Lucifer said when the remaining light caught the edges of his face just right. He wore black and gold, brocade and velvet. I wasn't that great at history, but this was the fashion of two centuries ago, but with the modern touch of the costume design department of the kind of dark fantasy show Trony liked to watch, and Lucifer looked like the sexy villain.

"Hi."

He eyed me from top to bottom, from my red boots, along the gold trimmed seam of my red cape, lingered on the crotch of my wine-dark pants, lingered again at my red shirt, which, for some reason would only button to about the middle of my sternum, before finally looking into my eyes. His smile deepening, he stood, walked up to me, and held out his hand. "Count Lea Ligassi, brother-in-law to the deceased. And who might you be?"

I was feeling the role, boy, was I ever feeling the role. Or no, I was feeling like the tall, dark, and handsome man from the suspect list was trying to seduce me.

"I'm...Robin of RedGraves, the deceased's nephew, and as I said, hi."

Lucifer chuckled, shook my hand, and held on to it so he could draw circles with his thumb along my skin. "Ah, sweet Robin, like that small, fragile bird. The innocent ingenue, are you. Tell me, darling Robin, has your uncle kept you in a convent all this time, hidden away from all who might desire you?"

Okay, I could try to convince myself that Lucifer in the role of some wicked count wasn't sexy, but...yeah, this was Midwinter, and I might as well play the game.

I blinked up at him like I thought Robin might, but the blush was all my own. "Not a convent, just an all-boys' school. But you shouldn't speak to me like this.

What would your wife say?"

Lucifer cocked his head. "The lady died a year ago. How strange your uncle never mentioned it."

"Well, he was strange."

"Indeed, sweet Robin. Might I accompany you to the feast?"

I nodded, and Lucifer held out his arm to me. I hooked my wrist under, and we walked out of our room and along the twilight castle's hallways.

"I trust your journey here went well, Robin?" Lucifer asked.

"Uhm, sure."

Lucifer stopped abruptly and bent his head so he could whisper in my ear. "Babe, you can't be all mono-syllabic. People will think you are the murderer, and they will lynch you. Just play with your role a little. That'll make it more fun to play with you."

That set my face to approximately the same shade of red as the rest of my costume. Lucifer chuckled.

"Okay, fine, but also fuck you, Count Lea, and do you see how I actually get to say that? Count Lea?"

"Mmm, did the teachers at that boys' school never wash your mouth with soap, Robin? Did they never make you pull your pants down so they could slap your very fine butt until it was just the loveliest shade of pink?"

My heart thundered, and when my hole clenched—for no reason—I felt that damn plug again, and fuck. He needed to stop talking.

"Nope, liked me to speak my mind. It's a progressive place like that, you know. Uncle approved. No naked asses anywhere in sight."

"Your uncle should have taught you discipline, Robin. Who will do so now, I wonder, since he failed to?"

We were making or way down a staircase, this one a later stone addition to the older wooden parts of the castle.

"I'm fine, and I don't need anyone to teach me discipline," I said. "And my trip was fine. The train was fine."

Lucifer laughed. "And was the conductor checking your ticket also fine?"

I wondered what a spoilt brat like Robin would actually say and straightened my back. "The conductor was an old, backwards man who thought nice hair and a passable ass made him the hottest man in uniform on that train, and he was not. My uncle may be dead, but at least he left me a discerning taste, Count Lea."

"Is that so?" he said just when someone else came our way from the gallery.

Trony had never worn as little pastels as she was this Midwinter. Instead, she wore vintage riding pants, the ones that flared at the thighs, and of course, high boots that were polished to a shine. The outfit was made somewhat stranger by a short, dark brown fake fur jacket with a good half dozen gold brooches. She wore rings to match too.

"Hello," Lucifer said. "I am Count Lea Ligassi, brother-in-law to the deceased, and this sweet boy is the deceased's nephew, Robin of RedGraves. He came all this way from his boys' school just to attend the funeral."

Trony narrowed her eyes at us. "Yeah, we're doing that pretend stuff in a second, you two deviants, but if you think I didn't see the wet footprints in your room, you are very, very mistaken."

Lucifer sighed and cupped my ass. The suddenness made me jump and squeal a little.

"Trony, I had to. You know how seductive Nelly gets, especially when he's wearing a long coat and a thong and makes pretty eyes at me all day."

"I…I did not make fucking eyes at you, Beelzebug!" I said.

"Shh, that's Count Lea to you, my darling schoolboy virgin," Lucifer said.

"I am not a fucking virgin."

Trony snorted. "You're dressed like a virgin, and clearly, you are aiming to get laid at the wake," Trony said before glaring at Lucifer again. "You best let me watch while you make out with him, because I'm not sure how else I'll manage to forgive you for the floors."

"Ooh! Well, if that's truly the only way…"

"Are you two fucking kidding me?" I said.

Trony crossed her arms. "Nope, no joke. Also, I'm Hannah van Hunt, the deceased's groundskeeper. The meal starts in the grand dining room. I'll show you."

We walked down the corridors that were the newer part of the castle, past the library where I'd fallen in love with Lucifer all over again just a few days ago. I stopped and pulled free of the Devil's hold on me when we came to a window from which the access road was visible, the very same in which Persephone had found Abigail MacFarlane's body. I tried to make out that spot, but the snow had gone up all the way to the sign that marked the way to the castle, a good six feet, if not more. In a way, it was as if the white was claiming what had happened out there, and maybe that was what Midwinter was good for: calling the dark memories of the old year and laying them to rest so something new could begin.

Lucifer's hand on the small of my back pulled me out of my musings. "The Feast is waiting, Nelly," he said, breaking character himself. I was glad he had.

"Yeah, let's go."

THE DINING HALL was all splendor. More of the wreaths Persephone and I had made hung on the walls and above the mantle of the large fireplace where a fire crackled away happily. Candles and more evergreen and holly branches made up the table decorations, weaving between the food. We were not having a regular feast then, but a buffet, given that the plates were in a neat pile, but that was fine. Although…how was I supposed to know when the second course ended?

There was a coffin next to the table, which would have been really disgusting if the corpse inside had been the real deal, but it was a wicker corpse in there, and Persephone was standing next to it, wearing glasses and a long gray skirt with a starched white blouse.

"Poor Count Krampus," she said, sniffling a little into a white handkerchief.

I left Lucifer to look into the coffin. Wicker uncle Krampus even had horns and seemed scary, a lot like the perchten mask atop the holiday tree.

"He looks good, even in death," I said. "You are?"

"Madeleine Ash, the librarian," she said. "I organized all your uncle's books and papers, sometimes daily, if he asked it."

"Nephew," the dragon mother said. She wore a long dress that went all the way to her neck. It was a golden brown that very nearly matched her skin tone, and from my character description, I knew who she was.

"Aunt Gothel. The count's unmarried sister," I added

for the benefit of Lucifer and Metatron, who'd come closer.

Tiamat cleared her throat. "It's all right, Robin. You can call me a spinster. Because I am. Unmarried and good at weaving things."

"Marriages never last anyway," Lucifer said with drama.

"My condolences again on your dear wife's death, Count Lea," Tiamat said. "We may have only shared a father, but Belle got so much more pleasant once she married you."

Lucifer grinned. "Because she moved out?"

Tiamat shrugged. "And now, she's moved on."

Well, these people. Clearly, my fictional family was all bad apples.

Before they could insult each other more, Hades came into the room dressed in a black butler's uniform, and boy. I knew my alpha god cleaned up good, but so did broad chested Hades.

"Whoa," I said.

Lucifer's head swiveled around to me, and he narrowed his eyes. Persephone giggled. "Dressing up isn't so bad after all, is it?" she said while Lucifer growled.

"The same sight in a different light," I said.

Hades smiled at Persephone. He carried a tray with mugs, one for each of us, and whatever he'd put in there, the drinks were on fire.

Okay, that was one way to kick off this murder mystery.

"Thank you, Stefan," Persephone said and stepped forward to take the first mug.

"At least the fire will burn out the poison," Tiamat said.

"Poison, Auntie Gothel?" I asked.

Tiamat shrugged. "One never knows, and poison kills fast. Your aunt Belle died fast from what I know of her death. Or did she, Count Lea?"

"I miss her dearly, as I'm sure do you," Lucifer said. "But my beloved Belle had a hunting accident." He reached for two mugs and handed me one. "Just alcohol, Robin. Not something they teach you about at the boys' school, is it?"

"Oh, boys' school as in, with a real uniform and plenty of exploration after lights out?" Metatron asked.

But the dragon mother—Aunt Gothel—put a hand on my shoulder. "Not for Robin. When he selected a school for Robin, Krampus made it very clear his behavior had to be exemplary, and his virtue intact." She smiled down at me. "Else he'd get the willow switch and would have ended in the sack."

"Auntie Gothel, I'm pretty sure that wasn't in the script," I said.

"Probably was in there between the lines," Metatron said and blew out the flame dancing atop her drink.

"I can't imagine he has ever known a man," Lucifer said and gave me another once-over, the slow kind, the hungry kind, the kind that made me very aware of the fact he had me plugged and caged. "Robin is very much not made of subtext, and his innocence shows."

Persephone cleared her throat, and Hades took the last remaining mug off the tray.

"If we could all focus on the here and now and drink to the memory of Count Krampus, the holiday beast we all loved so dearly?"

"Hear, hear," Lucifer said and blew out his drink.

I did too, and so did the others. We clinked our glasses

together.

"To Count Krampus," we all said and drank.

This was punch, strong because Hades had put some of his whiskey in it. It tasted a little different from the one he'd made when we'd done the holiday cookie baking, and I imagined I could taste pomegranate juice in it. It might have been just a different whiskey though.

After the first sip, the dragon mother walked toward the coffin. "And may tonight reveal who killed my dear brother. May justice find the vile murderer and see them punished for their crime."

Clearly, the game was on.

CHAPTER SIX
LUCIFER

IT WAS GOING TO BE DIFFICULT, WINNING THIS GAME AND not burning Nelly's clothes off and taking him right where he stood, but damn. He was distracting.

After the toast, we gravitated toward the table for what was clearly the first course, but I held Nelly back. I'd looked around the room, and there was very little time left for me to get the most out of him in terms of enjoying him playing his role.

"Say, Robin, would you tell me a bit about this painting?" I asked, walking up to a boring landscape that had probably gone for a lot at auction. Sometimes I was glad Trony didn't allow paintings into the house unless they had naked people in them.

"Well, I don't really know—"

"Oh, my," I said and looked up. "It would appear you've stepped under a mistletoe branch."

He frowned but followed my gaze. "Gee. What coincidence."

"And we have a deal, of course."

My necromancer cocked his head. "Yeah, I wonder; does that hold if there are no proper courses?"

Technically speaking, he had a point, but it wasn't like this was a deal he'd *want* to break. I was quite sure he'd enjoy a little bit of squirming and the freedom to let out his more stubborn self his role afforded him.

"I wonder if you'd really resist me if I dragged you to the powder room with me right this minute. Robin."

The look he got gave me my answer. Mmm. Maybe I should drag him off, but I was the Devil. I couldn't very well break a holiday tradition. And the mistletoe was right above our heads.

"Kiss the virgin already," Trony said, her plate piled with a colorful selection of simple oven roasted vegetables and one broccoli stuffed puff pastry.

"Come here, Robin," I said.

"This is inappropriate," he said. "I am grieving for my uncle, Count Lea, and you are being rude."

Trony started munching down on her food while she watched. Being watched was a bit of a turn-on, but it would be even more of one if there were less clothes involved.

"Robin, if nothing else, traditions help us cope with unexpected losses. And you are not alone. All of us are here because Count Krampus meant something to us. Though why he hid you away in that convent of a school, I cannot fathom."

Nelly rolled his eyes, but said, "Well, he wanted me pure, you know. I guess he really would have hated if, I don't know, I'd lost my virginity to someone called Marc."

Trony chuckled and I growled. Oh, here was my stubborn necromancer all right.

"I think it more likely he wanted to deny you the feel of a real man. With a real cock. Tell me, Robin, you know what a cock is, yes? You have been taught that much, or do they deny you biology class as well as one-on-one tutoring?"

Nelly sipped some more of his punch. "Cock as in rooster, you mean? Do you have a rooster in your pants, Count Lea?"

Trony was trying hard not to let the food spill out of her mouth with laughter. Who would have thought Nelly would enjoy a little game like this? I would definitely have to give a murder mystery of our own some thought.

I pulled Nelly close and took his chin in my hand. "Sweetest Robin, you seem thirsty for what I have in my pants. Now open your mouth as if you were about to sing a melody in music class."

Nelly hesitated in that way that always got to me, that way that made me want to have him and claim him. After that small defiance, he tilted his head back and let his mouth fall open.

I cupped his ass and made the kiss slow and sensual. A prelude. During it, I fantasized about how nice it would be to have him all to myself tonight—have him all to myself for the longest night—to truly draw out and enjoy all his little gasps, but each time I licked along his soft lips, I knew that wasn't something I could have, maybe not for the next few years.

Nelly had never had this, a family with which to play a lighthearted game to make the longest night seem less long, people who teased him without wanting to hurt him, people who cared and did things so he was happy. And even occasionally dropped him into a well or an oubliette, for his own good, of course.

I was no fool. Sephy liked planning, not as much as Trony, but a spontaneous murder mystery party was not Sephy's thing. She'd made it her thing the day after

Michael had shown up and attacked all of us, Nelly in particular. This game, it was for Nelly more than anyone else.

So in the end, even though I didn't want to relinquish the warm lips and the pleasantly sour taste that never let me forget Nelly's powerful necromancy, I released him, planted one last kiss on his lips, and brushed the flushed cheeks with my thumbs.

"I daresay someone taught you how to kiss at that school of yours, Robin," I said.

"Hot," Metatron commented. "A good start."

"Hmm," Nelly said as he slowly blinked up at me. He looked dazed. It would be so easy to get him from here to utmost pleasure, but that wouldn't be right. He'd have all the joys of Midwinter in the arms of our family tonight.

"Well, well, well, Count Lea," Tiamat said, sauntering over with a raspberry parfait in hand. "Are you seducing my nephew?"

Hades cleared his throat. "If ye are, would you like a selection of finger food with that?"

He held out a tray of the puff pastry things and some mini pizzas.

"Actually, food sounds amazing," Nelly said and went straight for two of the pizzas before wandering off to the table to get more food. And clear his head? Oh, I did not want him to clear his head.

But while he was gone, I could see about winning the game. "You seem very focused on your nephew's well-being, Gothel."

Hades walked off, but not completely out of earshot. As the butler, he could go wherever he wanted, and the butler was the murderer in a lot of these. Mmm. But close family was so much more likely. If I had learned nothing else from accompanying Nelly to his police work, I had learned that the closer people got to one another in their frail, human relationships, the more likely they were to despise each other and turn toward murder.

"Of course I care for my Robin," Tiamat said. "He is all that I have, after my brother's death, and after my sister." She smiled at me over her parfait. "But you have nothing at all, Count Lea, or isn't that right? Not after Belle's death. You are destitute, are you not?"

Now, *that* was supposed to be a well-guarded secret. And according to my character description, I should have been angling for a marriage with either Gothel or Robin, but clearly, Gothel was not amenable. At all.

"Are you accusing me of anything, Gothel?"

Before Tiamat could answer, the lights went out. This was part of the game and was supposed to make it more interesting. The magic also dimmed the fire as well as stealing everyone's sight except for the murderer. I could have cheated and found a loophole in the blindness spell, but that would not have been any fun.

"Robin! Where are you? Follow my voice," I said and started walking toward the table with the coffin next to it, arms out in front of me.

"Stay away from Count Lea, nephew," Tiamat said.

"I shall find candles," Hades said.

Right. Candles. If someone found and lit a candle before the time of darkness was up, we all had an actual chance to catch the murderer. Red-handed, if we were quick enough.

"Robin, come to me," I said as I felt around. This wasn't too bad, playing at human sight for a while, and Hades' spell was well-made enough to allow it.

"Count Lea? Where are you?" Nelly said from back

at the table.

"Don't—" Tiamat said, but before she could tell her nephew off for already having fallen for the handsome count—and so what if he came as the sole heir of his uncle's wealth?—the lights went back on.

"Candle," Hades said, holding up a single white one which he'd apparently found somewhere on the mantle.

"Oh, bloody murder," Metatron said, and the angel had a candleholder in hand. She stood by the table. And was a little bit too close to Persephone, who was lying on the floor and looking very fetching as the librarian's corpse.

Unlike a corpse, Sephy broke character for a moment to lift her head off the floor. "For the record, next time we do this, you can't kill me first, whoever you are, vile murderer." On her chest, there was a red cross, marking her out as dead. The thing even bled a little to add that much more realism.

I pushed past Hades and walked toward Nelly, who stood there with wide eyes and a half-full plate.

"Robin, are you well?"

Tiamat rounded on us. "It was either him," she jabbed at my forearm, "or the groundskeeper."

Trony rolled her eyes. Before she could respond, Cerberus came into the room, one head looking to all of us, the other two sniffing Sephy curiously. She reached up and scratched one head behind his ears.

"Lass, ye're dead," Hades whispered so loud everyone could hear.

"Well, I just crossed the Styx and am now making friends with the local wildlife," Sephy said. "Plus, as we discussed earlier, ghosthood doesn't have to be dull."

I chuckled.

"What do we do now?" Nelly asked.

Tiamat took a step back. "Krampus said he had to tell me something before he died. He said there was something important he needed to discuss, something only he and his trusted librarian knew."

"Séance?" Trony asked.

"Lass, that ain't in the rules," Hades said.

"Such a shame," Sephy said as Cerberus rolled on his back so she could scratch his belly.

"Maybe if we locked the suspect in a room until the police can get here?" Hades said and narrowed his eyes at Trony.

"Oh, no. This was not me," she said. "I was just trying to light the candles."

Nelly went about eating some of the food on his plate, and I took a step back. I liked feeding him a lot, liked him licking my fingers, but at the same time, he needed his strength. The first course was almost over, and before the second one started, I would need to ask him to show Count Lea where the bathroom was. And then Count Lea would reveal that he did not have a rooster in his pants.

Tiamat looked at Hades.

Nelly cleared his throat. "We can't lock her in a room because that would make it easier for the true murderer to kill her, and besides, we were all trying to get the lights back on, so that explains the candleholder," he said to Tiamat. "But thank you for the suggestion, Stefan. Auntie Gothel, did Krampus tell you anything else?"

"No, nephew," she said and brushed out her boring dress, although it did a nice job of showing her curves.

"The library then," I said. "Miss Ash was the librarian after all, and it stands to reason that whatever Krampus wanted to discuss might be there."

"Okay, if we are doing a scene change, I am getting up and haunting you all," Sephy said.

"Yer hot as a librarian, even hotter as one's ghost," Hades said.

She grinned at him. "Put another log on the fire before we leave. I'll watch."

I licked my bottom lip. "While you do that—will you show me the bathroom, Robin? I need to splash my face with some water after that kiss."

Nelly licked some creamy filling off his own lips, and my mouth watered at the sight. But I needed to maintain my role as well as get him alone, because it wouldn't do for me to lose this game, not when I'd been hanging around him and the other police people all this time. I should be able to solve this in my sleep by now.

Tiamat sighed and poured herself some eggnog from the pitcher on the table. "Mind your virtue, Robin. It was so important to poor dead Krampus over there."

"Should have bought his nephew a chastity belt," Trony said.

Nelly blushed, clearly remembering his caged cock.

Ah, what a lovely game this was.

"Follow me," he said and put his plate down before leading me to one of the bathrooms on this floor.

The moment his hand was on the handle, I brought out my wings, stalling him completely, and I pressed close to him and pushed us both into the bathroom.

The bathroom was generous with an anteroom with mirrors above the two sinks, and past that, two toilet stalls. From what Hades had told me, this had been a tourist place before he'd bought Sephy the castle, and they'd kept some of the features, for instance, this bathroom, and had made it fancier by adding the armchair and a selection of cosmetics along with a small bookshelf and an inexplicable cuckoo's clock on the wall opposite the mirrors.

"Babe, you are so hot in your costume," I said, pulling Nelly close. Sweet fuck, I wanted him.

"Count Lea, this is inappropriate," he said.

Correction, I wanted him *more*. Nelly was my desire always, but Nelly playing an innocent schoolboy? I was lost. But I could be the older man, initiating this schoolboy in the ways of pleasure.

"It's not, Robin," I said as I buried my hand in his hair and kissed him. "This is nature's will."

I rubbed against him. I felt his cage underneath his red pants, and he could feel me because I was so hard that there was no way he wouldn't. I kicked the door shut and pushed him farther into the room and pulled my wings open, then spun him around.

"Look at yourself, Robin." I was right behind him, my wings outstretched. He looked at himself, at my hands on him, at my feathers. This would be a little difficult for my necromancer, I knew, because I very much doubted he'd ever watched himself taking a cock. I doubted he'd ever done anything like what I had in mind.

Well, that was about to change tonight.

"C-count Lea, what are you doing?" he asked when I unbuttoned his shirt, not that it covered a lot. I considered removing his cloak briefly, but I liked it. It was not the coat I'd gotten him to wear over his lingerie, but more revealing and somehow enticing in a whole different way. If Sephy didn't let me keep this one, I'd get Nelly another cape to play with later.

"Oh, you must know what this is," I said. "The boys at school talk, don't they? They must have told you how men have needs and how a milk pale morsel like yourself will get things flowing, will rouse needs otherwise hidden and controlled."

I had his shirt open. I wanted to be inside him badly, but I wouldn't be able to last very long, not that we had all the time in the world for this, because I still would have to win the game. But I took a moment. To feel him through his pants, massage his ass so the plug was jostled, rub over his cage, something he would feel and have to react to…which he did.

He gasped, and perspiration beaded on his forehead. I nudged him forward so he could hold on to the counter in front of him. He curled one hand into a fist and had the other palm flat on the marble.

"Count Lea, but you were married to my aunt. You should still be in mourning, and I am…like my aunt said, my late uncle wouldn't want me doing this."

I bent to take his right earring between my teeth and pulled slightly. In the mirror, his pupils went wide, and his mouth fell open. Oh, it would have been tempting to make him kneel now and make him swallow, but there was bound to be more drinking, which meant I'd have to practice abstinence from my necromancer until he was sober again and fully able to appreciate me and all my hellish attributes. Simply put, I wanted to come in his ass again, because I wouldn't be able to for the next few hours after this.

I released his earring and kissed the spot behind his ear. He watched in the mirror, transfixed.

"You are family to me, Robin. My sweet, innocent Robin. I cannot imagine taking anyone else but you after my loss. As a matter of fact, I haven't had anyone after the loss of your aunt, and I… You see, Robin, it is difficult to bear. You'll make it easier, won't you? You'll help me, won't you, my darling nephew-in-law? By soothing this ache." I ground my hard cock into him, hitting his plug by how he moaned and shivered.

"Count Lea, you can't…"

"Of course I can, sweet Robin."

"But you shouldn't."

I grinned at him through the mirror. "I need the relief you are sure to bring me."

I worked his pants open finally and pushed them down along with the thong, once more just enough so I could have him. The best thing about this was watching Nelly watch himself, see himself caged and my hands roaming over his perfect, half naked body.

"But uncle," he said in the sweetest voice.

And that gave me an idea. "Touch yourself for me, Robin," I told him.

"W-what?"

I closed my hand around his caged cock and teased the tip through the metal. "Here. Touch yourself. Feel yourself. Go on. I'll tell you if I like what I see, and if I do, there'll be a reward."

He hesitated. He looked at me in the mirror, the playacting slipping away just for a moment to show his insecurity, but then he simply submitted. I loved watching him go through the resistance only to finally give in to this. To me. Give in to us, because I knew, for him, this was what it was, opening up and making himself vulnerable in a way he would have found impossible two months ago.

He reached for himself, working his erection through the cage, not an easy thing to do, and not anything that would get him off. That's what the cage was made for, after all, to ensure he could get aroused, very aroused, just not enough to readily release.

"Yes, like that. You keep doing that. Very nice." I kissed his temple. "Robin, play with your balls a little. There, that feels nice, doesn't it?"

"It…it feels strange."

"Really?" I reached down and ran a finger over his plug. "You'll get used to it. To having a man's cock inside you. After the first time, you'll need some training to take it well, but eventually, you'll crave it. Crave the feeling of being full. We really won't be able to send you back to that school of yours once you've been able to develop a taste for this," I said, and with that, I pulled out the plug. "If we did, you'd just spread your legs for all the other boys."

"Fuuuck," he said and bent forward over the sink counter.

"Very soon. No magic, babe." I prepared him, but he didn't need much. I'd left him ready, after all, and once more, that fantasy of keeping him like that all the time made me tingle all over, Nelly, wearing a dildo shaped like me, never wearing more than a shirt or a thin pair of pants. If he ever allowed me a wish, I'd ask him to do that for me, at least for a weekend. Maybe a long weekend.

I buried my nose in his hair before I tangled my fingers in the strands and pulled carefully.

"Robin, I want you to watch. Look at yourself. See what it does to you"—I lined up as soon as I had his attention.—"when you take a cock like mine."

I pushed inside him, and he did watch. Fuck, but for some reason, this was almost as hot as having him tied to our bed. Did I need to ask Trony to get me a few more mirrors? I probably should, just in case.

Nelly's tonsils were almost out and on display, that's how much he enjoyed this, and when I pulled back and thrust deep, he arched his back and let his eyes fall shut, the cape fanning over his back and sides.

"No, keep your eyes open. Watch yourself as you take my cock," I said.

He did as he was told, and there was that side of him, the Nelly that wanted to obey and please me. That was a drug, and I was a devil with a serious addiction problem.

"Lucy," he said, and that did it.

I used my magic to open his cock cage and reached forward to pull it off him.

"No more touching yourself now, babe, but keep watching," I told him, and he did, eyes drawn to his flushed cock.

I beat my wings to get his attention, and when his golden eyes were on me, I let go.

Bathroom sex was typically a fast and rough affair and somewhat dirty, which was the whole appeal. This— fucking Nelly as hard as I dared—was not dirty at all, but the mirrors made it something that pulled me along, as if the polished glass itself were magic and I nothing but a human who had to succumb.

And succumb I did, right when Nelly came, his cock bobbing from me rocking into him, then spurting, over his hands, over the sinks, making a glorious mess. I slammed everything I had into him, adding more to the cum that he'd already taken, and damn, breeding him like this was the best thing.

When his panting eased, he still trembled and steadied himself against the sink.

I pulled out. "Don't move, sweet. I'll clean you up." I reached for his chin and tilted his head back for a lazy kiss. "You did so well, you know that? Did you see how well you did, hmm?"

"Stop," he said, no force behind the word. "I'm not…"

I zipped my own pants back up and reached for a hand towel.

"You are perfect," I said and ran it under warm water. "You always are and always were."

I steadied him by the arm and wiped our combined juices from where they were already running down his thighs, which, frankly, was a look I liked on him: messy with the mess I'd made on him, in him, all over him.

"Don't say stuff like that," he said and bent his head to look at the backs of his hands.

"Mmh, why not, babe?"

"Because…" He turned around, awkward because of the pants around his ankles, but I steadied him. He lifted his golden eyes, and there was something in there that I had rarely seen but loved straight away: steady-handed esprit and a dash of cunning. "Because I have to murder you, and it makes me feel bad."

He marked a cross on my chest with two swift strokes, the enchanted chalk trailing red, before I could so much as beg for my life, not that I would have done any such thing.

"Ooopsie, you're dead," he said and grinned at me.

I looked at the cross. It bled a little, the fresh red adding more oomph to the scenery of murder. Such a nice spell.

"Babe, did you just turn me into a ghost?"

"Sure did. Count Lea, may he rest in peace."

"You used your wiles to seduce me," I said.

He shrugged, looking smug. "Didn't need any wiles.

You did all that yourself, falling for a hot schoolboy."

I sighed and folded my wings away. "Well, before I go about rattling my chains, you may want to search my pockets."

His eyebrows went up, but he did as I'd told him, going for the right one first, which was when I realized I had Ariadne's damn coin in there, and I didn't want him to touch that.

"Other one," I said.

He gave me a quizzical look but went for the left pocket. And pulled out another pair of underwear, this one nice panties with lots of lace on his butt cheeks and some see-through material in the front. These were black, and they made a nice contrast to his all-red attire.

He held it up between us. "For real?"

I shrugged. "You said you wanted a change of underwear, and we have a deal. This is me holding up my end of it."

"These are transparent. They can barely be classified as underwear."

I shrugged. "By all means, go commando, my love. I don't mind."

He frowned prettily. "You are not making me wear fancy lace panties until the new year, Beelzebug," my once more contrary necromancer said.

"Mmm, we'll see. Now go ahead, Robin, put on your new things." I walked over to the chair. "I'll be haunting you from right here."

I watched him frown and huff and snatched the thong when he slid that off and kindly tossed it my way, which made me wonder what it would take to train him to strip for me.

He slid the panties on, and with his lovely pale skin,

the black worked wonderfully, and I liked the contrast it created with the red. The lace hugging his butt was equally enticing, and it made me wonder whether instead of angling to chain him to the bed, I should instead endeavor to make a deal which resulted in him having to wear nothing but whatever I picked for him. Mmm. There was an idea.

Before he even had a chance to stuff his shirt back into his pants, the lights went out again.

"Fuck, I need to find someone to murder," my necromancer said.

Ah, it was so rewarding to be present when people found their true calling.

CHAPTER SEVEN
LIONEL

Lucifer had been the easiest kill. I could have murdered him straight away, but then everyone would have suspected, and if they all agreed and searched me and found my magic chalk, I'd lose. Or if they put me in the coffin with Uncle Krampus, that also was a lose condition.

Seriously, who had thought up *that* rule?

The darkness was fun. I had to ask Hades how he had made the spell. The world was shades of gray, like an old holiday movie, and when I opened the bathroom door, I hoped it would take them some time to find candles to banish their blindness, because candles did not belong in the library.

But I got even luckier than that. Hannah van Hunt—Metatron—was just outside the door.

"Fuck," she said when she heard me come out, but she was blind, and for once, having an advantage over everyone else's magic was pretty sweet.

I didn't hesitate and closed the distance between her and me in three long strides before X-ing her chest.

"Got you," I said.

"I knew it," Metatron said, but got to the floor like the rules demanded.

"Your knowledge dies with you, Hannah van Hunt," I whispered to her, then dropped my chalk next to her hand and went back into the bathroom where the boyfriend unit was still sitting in the fancy chair. Where he was idly sniffing my discarded thong and making his Devil sounds.

"If you want to play a corpse, start now so I can drag you outside," I told him.

Lucifer's eyes were still bright, a shimmery silver-gray, but I liked that he couldn't really see me. I had no doubt that he could have manipulated the spell if he'd wanted to, but it was nice that he stayed put.

"Babe, you're a shrimp, and I'm a mighty killer whale. You cannot drag me anywhere."

"You're too chatty for a corpse, and I'm a murderer who needs to cover up his crime so he can do more crime." I looked at the feet of the armchair. They had those woolly floor protection stickers on them, and before he could distract me more, I rounded the armchair and just pushed as if I were giving birth or something.

"Oh, that's crime-savvy," he said.

"Chatty corpse."

"Talking to a necromancer, babe. I feel entitled to your attention now that I have passed on to a very long future of haunting your every waking moment."

We were close to the door. If he wasn't going to get out of that chair, he wasn't going to like how I was going to get him out of it.

"You're already doing that."

"And you like it."

Well, yes, I did. I'd known that for a good long

while, but it was just such a new thing, this…emotional intimacy between us. It felt a little bit like a fresh wound you couldn't leave alone but knew you had to so it would heal, except instead of pain and blood, what Lucifer and I had now was love…and trust. And I'd thought loving him would be scary. Trusting him was scarier, but I would face my fears. And I would even work out how I could show him that and become someone he'd also want to trust.

After I'd gotten him out of the chair.

I stopped to open the door, pushed the chair forward another foot.

"Oh, the excitement," Lucifer said.

Metatron snorted. "You may be excited. I almost had him."

"You weren't sure it was me," I said to the angel on the floor.

"No, but it was either you or Lucifer, or you were working together, and I was so close to putting you two in a coffin," she said.

"Got a bit too close. So, uhm, Lucy, you need to get out of the chair."

"Babe. I am a ghost. Getting out of the chair serves no purpose in the development of a sexy haunting, which was what you said you wanted from me."

"I said no such thing but have it your way."

Tilting the damn armchair over was hard work, but I did it. Lucifer slid out and huffed, and Metatron groaned. I didn't think my move had been fast enough to surprise Lucifer, but it was still satisfying.

"I'm feeling used," Metatron said.

"Trony, but your costume is so soft," Lucifer said while I pushed the chair back where it belonged.

"No shrimp after all." I dusted off my hands, but there was no point in wasting time.

I jogged back to the door and closed it, turned the key in the lock, and dropped to my knees.

"Babe, I'm a ghost. I can pass through walls now."

"You got into his pants and let your guard down, didn't you?" Metatron said.

I chuckled because I could just imagine how that would fluster Lucifer. "Yes, he did. Totally went for the innocent schoolboy spiel."

The key barely fit under the gap between the door and the floor, but lucky for me, the castle was old, and there was a gap to begin with.

I took a deep breath, then hammered my palm against the door.

"Hello? Auntie Gothel? Count Lea, please let me out!"

The light was still off for everyone but me, but I hoped my voice would carry.

"Did you know he had that much potential for being a criminal?" Metatron asked, although I had to press my ear to the door to hear the two ghosts on the other side better.

"No. This Midwinter has been quite…revealing," Lucifer said.

"Ah! He likes the lingerie, doesn't he?"

Well, how in the name of fuck did Metatron know about the lingerie?

I was about to ask her when I heard Lucifer say, "He's wearing those black panties now, the organza ones."

"You two are supposed to be dead! Can you stop discussing my fucking underwear," I said.

They shut up, but not for long.

"You know, I think we need more mirrors in the bedroom," Lucifer said, and I decided I had heard enough.

I banged against the door with renewed vigor and screamed for my auntie.

"OH, LOOK! MORE corpses," Persephone said after the lights had gone back on.

"Aye, it's turning into a real haunted castle," Hades said.

I banged on the door again. "Hello? Let me out of here, please?"

"Where is—ah. Lad, are ye decent, or did he burn the costume off you?" Hades asked, proving that he knew Lucifer all too well.

"Fully clothed, Stefan, thank you very much," I said.

Lucifer's ghostly chuckling could be heard loud and clear before Hades turned the key in the lock and opened it.

"There you are, young master Robin," Hades said, his silvery eyes twinkling.

I bit my bottom lip, looked past him, and took a few steps back.

"Did you murder Count Lea and Hannah, Stefan?" I asked.

I didn't see the dragon mother, but Persephone was craning her neck to look around Hades. Cerberus had followed, and at least two of the three heads looked at us like we'd lost our minds, running around the castle and screaming when there was a table full of food. Metatron and Lucifer were on the floor, sitting cross-legged, though Metatron had gotten herself some cherry and cream cake at some point. Was there cherry cake? I needed me some of that too. Murder was such hard work.

"I did not," Hades said and walked into the bathroom after me.

I stepped back again, and Persephone walked in past Hades and sat down in the very chair I'd tossed my boyfriend the Devil out of not all that long ago. She was grinning. I wasn't sure whether she knew I was the murderer because I'd just acted as fast as I could with her, but she had to know Hades wasn't it.

The question was, would I have to act, or was the dragon mother going to?

"You were on the other side of the door, standing over them," I said.

"Master Robin, I just serve drinks and food. What reason would I have to wish anyone dead?"

I snorted. "We'd need to ask the librarian that, wouldn't we? But you murdered her before we had a chance to do just that. You would have been in the room when my uncle and she discussed whatever it was that was so important."

I saw the hem of a brown dress by the door, but this was going to be tricky. I couldn't let Hades know Tiamat was out there.

"I've served your uncle for all my life, lad, and I'm all set to serve you as well, now that his estate is yours."

Which was when the dragon mother struck, marking Hades' back with a red cross with the chalk I had placed outside the door.

"Ah, bullocks," he said. I had no idea what being killed in the game felt like, but he looked over his shoulder and turned so he could see his red mark in the mirrors above the sinks.

I let out a sigh of relief. "Thanks, Auntie. He murdered Uncle, but he never said why."

Hades grumbled and rolled his eyes. In order to finish the game if the murderer was found, we'd have to discover the motive in order to win, that's what the rules said.

"Come to my side of the veil, my beloved!" Persephone said.

"It's really getting crowded on this side of the veil," Metatron said.

Tiamat stayed in character. "We need to find out why he murdered everyone."

Honestly, it was a lot like a murder investigation, this, including the little detail that you could be wrong about who the murderer was.

I nodded and did my best to look shaken. That came easily enough when I thought about what Lucifer had done to me. How he'd looked, all wild and powerful, behind me and in me, and thrusting into me while his muscles coiled—yeah, that was enough to make me feel all kinds of shaky.

Tiamat was either mindreading me or just guessing because she looked at Lucifer, who was watching, sort of enthralled, eyes on me and dipping to my low-cut shirt every so often.

"I see Count Lea is dead. Did he take advantage of you, nephew?"

I had no idea whether this was in her character, or whether she was doing something nice for Lucifer, but I decided to play along. It wasn't an easy decision, and it wasn't my knee-jerk reaction, but…I was in love with Lucifer, I really, truly was, and he'd probably enjoy the fuck out of this.

"He…he said it was natural. And that real men have needs. He said he would show me things no one ever showed me back at school."

Yup, that had been the right decision. Lucifer's sapphire eyes heated, and he looked like he wanted to rise from the dead and bend me over the sink all over again. But I was the only necromancer here, and I wouldn't allow him back from death. At least not before I had murdered my Auntie Gothel and had gotten all the inheritance.

Tiamat as Gothel sighed. "That is too bad. Your uncle was a firm believer in someone pure inheriting after him. We shall have to find a good match to marry you off to now."

"But, Auntie Gothel…" Hah! She had no idea my dead aunt Belle had told me as much in the last letter I'd received from her before her mysterious death. And that death probably was a whole other murder mystery and not just a simple hunting accident.

Tiamat put the red chalk down on the sink counter and turned on the water, because the chalk did stain. Good thing I was wearing all red.

"It will be fine, Robin, dearest."

"I guess it will," I said and did my best to look innocent.

I took a neatly folded hand towel off the shelf by the wall and held it out to Tiamat in such a way that it covered the chalk, and when she reached out to take it, I snatched the chalk and pretended to stumble. She reflexively opened her arms, and I marked the very center of her chest with a bright red cross that shimmered like the fire we had going in the dining room.

"No! Not you, young one," Tiamat said.

The lights flared three times, and chimes rang

through the air. I grinned. I'd never won anything, and I couldn't really remember the last time I'd played a game with anyone. At the Collegium, the magic users who played card games never invited me because I was good at keeping track of cards, and the ones who played magic games never invited me because I was too good at all of them, given the strength of my magic. The mages had never invited me because I wasn't one of them.

"The lad lured me and murdered me in cold blood," Hades said and came forward to clap me on the shoulder.

"Oaf. Nelly is delicate, so please don't break him," Lucifer said, swooping in to embrace me, kiss me deep, and cop a feel, of course. Because he had to make sure the damn lingerie fit nicely on my ass, no doubt. "Well done, babe. You killed them all."

"He sure did," Persephone said. "I wasn't sure it was him because I didn't even see him come at me. He struck like a rattlesnake, and then stood there, eating finger food like nothing had happened."

"Like a necromancer about to ram his magic wand through your heart," Metatron said before she stuffed the last bit of cake in her mouth.

"We call that an athame, and it's not how anyone does magic," I said.

"Oh, they did, a long time ago, young one. Now that we are all dead and that young Robin here is the sole heir of the Krampus fortune, should we all go back to our Krampus feast?"

Everyone agreed. I was glad. I needed some of that cherry cake.

ON OUR WAY back to the dining room, Lucifer and I stopped by the great room with the holiday tree to check on Soul and the babies.

Soul growled in greeting when she saw me. She was lying on her side, and the babies had fallen asleep right there, close to her, their three unusual tails trembling as they dreamed.

I sat on the floor next to their nest and scratched Soul behind the ears before running my hands over Murray and Quincey.

"They look so peaceful."

Lucifer slid to one knee next to me. "Why wouldn't they be? After all, they didn't just commit mass murder like this necromancer I could name."

He stroked the babies too and tugged the bedding of their nest over them, although I didn't think they were cold. The fire was stoked and the flames licked up into the dark chimney. Combined with the magical orbs that flowed around the big-ass tree, it gave the room a comfy golden light.

"I didn't think winning against you all would be that easy," I said. "After all, you're supposed to be good at games, according to the legends."

He frowned at me. Oh boy. Was I getting close to harming the fickle and fragile alpha god ego again?

"For one thing, those are human myths, and they are—more often than not—made of horse manure with a sprinkling of pure and unadulterated idiocy. For another thing, I am more than happy to concede my win to you."

Concede, my ass. "Perhaps I'll let you win next year," I said, my tone light.

"And perhaps I'll burn all your clothes so you have to stay indoors, wearing nothing but your beautiful underwear and your new coat."

I bit my lip, but I couldn't resist. "Even if you do that, Beelzebug, I'll still have murdered you in a bathroom."

Lucifer grinned at me. "Keep that spirit for when we go and beat Winston and his partner at bridge next year. If you do well, I'll reward you."

"Can't get out of that, can I?"

He leaned into me and kissed me tenderly. "No."

We stayed there a few more minutes before heading back to the feast.

The room had changed. The first thing I noticed was Cerberus, mostly because the left head was ignoring me. He stared up at the table, up at the cheese plate, three noses sniffing, three sets of eyes doing their best at telekinetically making the cheese roll off the table. After all, Cerberus had not been fed at all through the year, and no one ever gave him even the smallest treat, so he did not have the strength to even attempt stealing cheese off the table, not that he would, given that he was the best at behaving, and if he were fed, he'd behave even better.

The coffin with dearly departed Uncle Krampus had been moved away from the table and was now sitting on a small pyre of chopped wood. Underneath all that, I spotted a tarp, and when I headed over there and reached for it to see how it was spelled, I felt the divine magic it had been imbued with.

"It's so it doesn't burn everything," Hades said. He was adding more logs to the pyre.

"Wait. Are we burning this thing? Inside?"

Metatron, in the process of helping Persephone and the dragon mother put the chairs and place sets back around the table, stopped for an annoyed groan.

"Yes, we are," she said. "Because we are in the

company of *delicate* human wildflowers and murdery necromancers, and they cannot be taken outside in the snow for a small bonfire."

The dragon mother patted Metatron's arm. "This will also be easier, given it's still snowing. Even I got buried under the fresh snow a few times when I was snowbathing earlier."

Lucifer had found a large basket with pinecones somewhere and put that down next to me.

"And Nelly was already outside earlier today and complaining about how his delightfully firm butt was getting hypothermia. I would not dare risk that again."

The ass grinned at me like he wanted to say, *Oh, canary, come here and make me stop.*

"You were gone quite a long time," Persephone said. She was turning on burners on which several of the dishes sat to warm them up, although most of the feast could be eaten cold. My knowledge of history, or at least of the history of Midwinter celebrations, wasn't that good, but if the feast was supposed to last all through the night, having a lot of cold dishes made sense.

"Lucy helped me with something," I said, then looked at the Devil. "Again, thanks. I couldn't have done that thing without you."

"He helped you with ruining my floors and the freshly washed linen, is what he did," Metatron grumbled.

The dragon mother clicked her tongue. "Trony, I assume they will be very horny for each other for the next long while. You know that's how these things go."

"Aye," Hades said. "And sometimes the horniness never ends, or isn't that right, lass?"

Persephone nodded. "So very right. Especially when I get to watch you take apart a yule log. For the life of me,

I can't remember why we stopped with those."

Hades grunted and headed over to kiss her deeply. "We'll reinstate it then."

"Wonderful," Lucifer said. "That means I get to cut down the Christmas tree next year as well, doesn't it?"

"Mate, you're an old cheater, and that's not how it goes." Hades crossed his arms and started a glaring contest with Lucifer.

Before this could end in another naked snowball fight in the chest deep snow out there, I tugged on Lucifer's jacket. He was still wearing the black and gold count outfit, and it made him look even more dapper than his urban chic tailored jeans and shirts did. The red crosses on everyone had almost faded completely now.

"I love the tree you picked this year. I've never seen anyone carry a tree that size by themself."

Lucifer fixed me in a sapphire stare. "Babe, the tree really wasn't that big," he said.

Did I have to rub his ego more? Better be safe. "I thought it was."

Metatron groaned while Persephone was whispering something to Hades, likely stuff about how he'd been so sexy, carrying the yule log home and then chopping it up all by himself.

The dragon mother ended the banter and ego soothing by clapping her hands.

"Someone crack a window and add a spell so the smoke doesn't ruin the ceiling in here," she commanded, and Metatron opened one of the top panes of the tall windows before adding a spell to the pyre I only noticed because I was expecting it.

"Good," the dragon mother said. "Now, young one, since you won our little game, you should get to light the bonfire."

Lucifer tapped the big basket of pinecones with his toe. "Use these."

I picked up a cone as everyone gathered around the pyre, around the Krampus of last year we were about to burn, presumably so the shorter nights could give way to brighter days.

"Does anyone have a lighter?"

"With your magic, lad," Hades said.

I eyed the cone. The only time I'd ever heated up anything was when they'd made me use a talisman back at the Collegium. I'd ruined a table, but even then, I hadn't made a fire.

But I had something now that I didn't have then.

I looked up at Lucifer. "Will you help me?"

His nostrils flared, and while he didn't move, something in him shifted, or at least that's the impression I got. It made my heart speed up and the skin on the back of my neck prickled with a primal reaction to his regard.

"Of course, my love. But just a little. You can do most of this yourself." He closed his hand around my own and the pinecone I was holding. "Feel my magic and follow it," he said. "You've done that before."

I had, back at a frozen pier, so I knew this would work. I knew I could trust him to show me what to do.

This time, he didn't help me visualize the magic like before, and the moment his magic touched me, a rush of comforting familiarity went through me. It was almost like when we made love.

He wasn't doing all the work for me, but he was leading me along as if making fire were a dance. I followed, and while this wasn't the easiest thing—he made me pour a lot of magic into the heart of the pinecone while holding it there—it wasn't as hard as figuring it out by myself would have been.

"Good. Don't worry about the flames, my love, I have you," he said, and my fingers and palm tingled with whatever spell he did.

Then he plucked the magic I kept contained in the pinecone, almost like plucking a string, and I knew what he wanted me to do. I did the same thing and released it, and the pinecone burst into bright flame in our hands.

Lucifer did magic to the flames, and they briefly went purple, then blue, then orange and green.

"Show-off," I said, and together, we tossed the pinecone on the pyre.

Well, we tossed it into Uncle Krampus's coffin, and just like a good wicker creature, he burst into flame.

Everyone clapped and oohed and ahhed. It really was a pretty fire.

I nearly jumped out of my skin when something licked my fingers, but Lucifer steadied me. With a hand on my ass. Seriously, did he always have to hold on to my butt?

"Just Cerberus, babe."

The leftmost head had done this, judging by how he licked his jowls. All three looked at me with imploring eyes. He yowled softly from three maws.

"Oh, you big bottomless hole," Persephone said and walked over to Cerberus. "Nelly is immune to your puppy dog eyes."

"Damn hellpooch is trying to impress the necromancer's alpha. It's pack behavior," Hades said.

"You know that all these alpha and beta wolf tales have been disproven by science? They only exist and thrive in romance novels these days," Metatron said.

"That's very true. But it's really the omegas everyone wants," the romance novel expert who still had his hand on my ass said.

"Maybe that's an angle for your murder mystery dinner party?" Persephone said to Metatron. "The guests have to find out who the omega is?"

Lucifer made his growly noises, and his hold on my ass tightened.

"Gods, can you unhand me?" I asked.

"No. And there's only one way to find out who the omega is."

"Fucking," Metatron said.

"Aye, fucking," Hades added, and the dragon mother nodded sagely.

"Well, okay, that might not work for a party setting then," Persephone said. "But you know what? We're burning our wishes in the bonfire."

She got stationery from a side table and handed out small notepads to all of us.

"You'll need to take your hand off me if you want to write," I said to Lucifer, because he still had not.

"Babe, I need to make sure there won't be any hypothermia, just like you asked me to," he said, holding his pad and pen on the flat of his palm, and magicked the damn pen to write by itself. "And I'm magic."

Smug was what he was.

"Please just get this done so we can finally start feasting," Metatron said.

"Always so pushy," Hades said but wrote.

I stared at the blank page. Did I have a wish? For a moment, I thought I knew what to wish for: to meet my mother. To speak with her like Lucifer had. I couldn't really help but feel a little bit jealous about that, and maybe I wanted her to tell me to my face why she'd abandoned me.

Then again, there was also Minos. I wasn't sure whether I'd ever have the strength to talk to him again, but I had thought about that. For a wish though, I'd want him to—for once in his long, long life—feel the terror he'd afflicted on others.

I didn't write down any of this though, even though this was just a ritual and probably meant nothing.

What did I want? I glanced sideways at the Devil, his shiny kitty-cat hair bronzed in the gleam of the bonfire. All I wanted could be summed up in a single word, not Lucifer, not Devil, no.

I spelled it out in all caps: BEELZEBUG.

CHAPTER EIGHT
LUCIFER

WE FOLDED OUR WISHY PAPERS INTO THE PINECONES, THEN tossed them to the hungry bonfire before sitting down around the feast table.

I could not remember a longest night that had been this short. Nelly started out by securing himself a big piece of cherry cake, but before he could quite sink his fork into the pink cream icing, Hades poured a round of Lethe.

"The eighteen-year-old, cheers," he said, and we all drank.

Nelly had finished half that drink—and all his cake—when Persephone said, "I wonder whether this snow will finally kill the rhubarb."

I knew that my necromancer was already on his way to tipsy when he started giggling and said, "You know, if Michael's sword didn't kill it, I don't think snow can."

Next, we moved on to the punch, a fresh batch also containing whiskey, and served once again with flames licking over its surface.

"I hope these are magical flames, Hades," I said and rubbed Nelly's back. He was currently enjoying Trony's risotto, the one with sage and pumpkin.

"Mate, you do not tell me how I light my damn punch. Do I come into your house and tell you how to get people naked and into your pretentious Jacuzzi? No."

"My Jacuzzi is *not* pretentious."

"Which one isn't, the indoor one, or the outdoor one?" my most traitorous necromancer asked without really taking his attention off the risotto.

Well, the next time I was getting him naked in the Jacuzzi, there would be no tasting of any type of liquor happening, and he'd recant any ridicule by the time I showed him how wonderful it was to be with a god who didn't need to breathe when he was underwater.

"Careful, with that one, Lucy," Hades said.

"Don't encourage him," I said through gritted teeth.

"I'm just eating rice here and having punch."

Cerberus whined, and so I accidentally dropped a few of the queer and rainbow sprinkled gingerbread people Nelly and Sephy had made.

"Philistine! First, you mess with my floors, then you dis my risotto, which is not just *rice*," Trony said from across the table. She had been talking about potato recipes with Sephy, and I was sure we were in for a few new variations.

Nelly's cheeks flushed. "What I meant was, this is the epitome of rice. It's what rice aspires to become."

"Hear, hear," the dragon mother said, and we all drank again.

Sometime past midnight, I had to make a conscious effort to somewhat moderate Nelly's punch intake. The last time he had fallen for overly sugary drinks, I hadn't been there, had only come in at the end of it, and it had resulted with him cozying up to a vile thing before being violently sick, at which point I had at least been present to take care of him.

By around one in the morning, Hades was once again recounting that first winter night we'd run into Loki in his horse form and pursued by a stallion. I'd have to get Hades to tell it again because Nelly was definitely flagging and leaning against me, his eyes falling shut on and off. I'd long since pulled his chair close to mine so he could lean against me.

An hour later, he was in my lap and dozing, his magic's sour vinegar and lemon scent blending with all the sweet punch and peaty whiskey he'd had. The dragon mother was talking about how she was remodeling her new house back in Brunswick, and I was reminded of my duty of building her a bird feeder come spring.

And of the snow shoveling. Not a week went by when I wasn't reminded of the damn snow shoveling. At least when there was yard work to do, I could let her and Nelly have tea on the patio, and then I'd pull my shirt off eventually, but Nelly wasn't made for being in the cold for long enough to watch me take off my winter clothing and not show the telltale signs of being too cold.

"Lucy, we are doing presents tomorrow morning, by the way," Sephy told me a little before three o'clock, the witching hour.

I liked the idea of that, and I nodded. The sooner the better.

When the witching hour rang—literally, because Hades had enchanted the small clock on the mantle to echo through the house like a large bell—we all got up and gathered around our little indoor bonfire again. I scooped up Nelly in my arms, but he blinked awake from his doze.

"What's going on?"

"The official part of the Midwinter Feast is done, my love." I set him on his feet and took the basket with the pinecones the dragon mother passed to me. "Take one more."

He did, and so did I before passing the basket on to Trony.

"It goes in the fire, young one. Not a wish for you, but one for those who are no longer here or for those who have no fire of their own this night," the dragon mother said. "It might be this tradition that modernity translated into Santa's list of naughty or nice children, but somewhere in the translation, making a selfless wish for someone else got lost."

I myself wouldn't have minded another wish. I'd have wished my Nelly fully sober, because holding him so close for the last two hours just left me aching to be even closer to him all over again.

My thoughtful necromancer rubbed his sleep-lidded eyes and stared at the pinecone in his hand. Hades and Sephy tossed theirs in as one.

"Merry Midwinter," they said in unison and headed for their bedroom hand in hand.

Tiamat and Trony tossed in theirs and left for their respective rooms, but Nelly stood there, a little lost, and when the last footsteps were gone, he still hadn't moved or said anything.

For once, I didn't need my wings to tell me what he was thinking.

The corpses of three young women he had raised here in Scotland over the past week. Three young women whose names he had brought back from the silence of death so their families wouldn't spend another Christmas with uncertainty. Nelly would not and could not see it that way. He would always see the dead he could do so little for, the dead who did not get to have another longest night with their loved ones. None of that was his fault, but Nelly, so very powerful but not powerful enough to unmake death, he blamed himself for it.

"The wishes will find the fire, you know. That's why we let it burn all through the night. All you have to do is toss it in," I said and cupped his neck.

He nodded, but still didn't say anything.

A friendly growl had me look down. Soul had joined us, her black eyes focused on Nelly, a string of drool connecting her jowls to the floor. Cerberus kept a respectful distance, but he was wagging his tail.

"Hey, you shouldn't leave the babies alone," Nelly said and went to his knees next to Soul so he could scratch her behind her floppy ears.

I left him to it, because he still seemed much too pensive, given the happily tipsy state he'd been in, right after he'd been so proficiently murderous.

After a while of cuddling Soul, he turned to the flames and tossed the pinecone in. It cracked and sizzled, and maybe, that wish came true. I tossed mine in straight after so that maybe a pair of wishes could be fulfilled through these flames.

When he stood back up, he was a little unsteady like the lightweight I knew him to be. Soul headed back off to her hellbrood, and I scooped Nelly up into my arms again.

"I can walk," he grumbled, although it was barely a complaint. "'S not that hard, walking."

"I know, babe, but don't do magic."

"Won't the castle burn down if we leave the fire

going?"

I chuckled. "The bonfire is warded, my love. A lot of everyday magic all around tonight."

I teleported us to our dark room. I didn't want to turn on the lights, but I didn't want Nelly to be fully lost and adrift either, so I brought out my wings for him.

Like he always did, his eyes went wide, and he stared, and because he had less inhibitions given his drunken state, he reached out and didn't pull back.

Joy. I felt joy inside him when he touched my feathers, a bittersweet joy because there was no other kind during Midwinter but joy all the same.

"What did you wish for? With your paper pinecone thingy," he asked.

I smiled at him and licked my lips. "Can't tell you. It's like birthday candles. You can't say what you wished for because if you do, it might not come true. Mmm, speaking of, do you want a surprise party for your birthday, or do you want to know I'm organizing one?"

He chuckled. "Was that why you really went to search for my birth certificate?"

"Oh, I knew what your birthday was long before that. Who do you think left the chocolate muffins on whatever work desk you currently occupied at the time for the past four years?"

His eyes widened, and his jaw dropped. Hmm. That one had finally paid off. I did like a slow burn that ended in a scrumptious reveal.

"No. You did not. Are you fucking kidding me? I thought Christine had done that."

I lifted an eyebrow. "No. I did."

"Son of a—motherfucker!"

"No, I strictly fuck you, babe. Soon. When you have

sobered up again. And maybe I'll make you put on the red cape for it. Nothing but the red cape." I was very glad I'd bought several pairs of lingerie in red for him. That too would pay off soon.

"How did you find that out though? I mean—really? You snuck into the police station with a fucking chocolate muffin—"

"Double chocolate muffin with a liquid chocolate core." Which I had baked myself, along with the small spell that kept the core velvety melt-on-your-tongue soft.

"Fine, whatever. You did *that*, and you didn't just fucking run into me and toss your hair around a little and *brag* about putting pastry on my desk?"

I had considered that, but my goal had been to get Nelly dreaming about a secret admirer so much so he'd end up obsessed. I'd hoped he'd try to enlist any and all supernatural help he could possibly muster in finding said admirer, meaning I'd hoped he'd come a-knocking on my door. I'd not expected him to attribute my good deeds to Christine, but that just went to show that I hadn't really known my necromancer all that well back then. I would not make any such mistake with him again, and in the end, he hadn't needed subtlety. All I'd had to do was inform him we were dating—combined with the magical exchange giving a favor provided—and romance had happened.

"I can be selfless, babe," I said because he didn't need to know all the other stuff. "And I never brag, I only ever state facts."

He snorted. "Well, fuck me."

"I will, soon. Now let's get you undressed and into bed."

He nodded. "Yeah, sleep. Fucking long night."

I chuckled. "The longest, babe."

He didn't resist or tell me off when I undressed him, and once I had him under the covers, I was quick to get out of my own costume and join him.

I closed my necromancer into my wings and felt him relax instantly, felt him sink into the certainty that he was safe—in my arms, in my bed, under my starlight wings.

I reveled in his trust and listened to his thoughts as he slipped away into dreaming. This was my Midwinter wish come true, after all:

"I wish for Lionel Ionos Hawkes, the love of my immortal life, to find nothing but happiness in the next 365 days and nights...and that I may be granted as many days of flawless kitty-cat hair so he can admire it."

EPILOGUE

THE DAY AFTER MIDWINTER

Lucifer

MORNING DIDN'T BREAK WITH MUCH SUNSHINE AT ALL, BUT I didn't care. I, the Devil, lay there with my dreaming necromancer wrapped in my arms, giddy with excitement like a human child on Christmas morning. The best thing was that I would get to give Nelly a Christmas morning on top of this morning after Midwinter. I imagined him being so completely overcome with joy that he'd tell me he wanted to make a wish of mine come true as well.

My cock filled rapidly at the idea of Nelly looking up at me with his pretty golden eyes and asking, "What do you want for Christmas, Lucy? I'll give you anything you want."

It would have to be him in my bed for the next several days of course. I imagined all the things I'd do with him and how he'd seek out my warmth and nearness after. It was a pretty little fantasy, and the way it kept going round and round in my mind was sweet torture.

Nelly woke late of course. It had been the longest night, but also a long day for him, what with the geese and the heretofore unknown penchant for murder.

I loved how soft and warm he always was in the mornings, and when he stretched, lazily blinked the sleep out of his eyes, and smiled up at me, I barely managed not to fall on him like a wild beast.

I kissed him, not saying a word because too much conversation before caffeination always led to a cranky necromancer. And words were not needed.

My kiss aroused him. I felt the spike of lust through my feather tips and chased it with my tongue and my hands stroking his body, coaxing him to open and relax.

There was no rush with this, no pressure, just him and me and the castle silent around us, the rest of the world buried in snow. He tasted of lemony vinegar and young grapes, his demigod magic close to the surface but not quite breaking through.

Nelly reached up to run his fingers through my hair, something he loved whenever I chose not to restrain his hands. Something he savored all the more for the fact that he knew he'd likely be tied up the next time we made love.

And he would be. I did enjoy him like this, his touches, not quite as shy as one would assume, not nearly as forward as I would have allowed him, but my preferred flavor would always be when he was willing to put himself into my hands completely. He was so utterly beautiful in his vulnerability whenever he did that, and my balls tightened when I remembered the last time I'd tied him to one of the bed posts one morning and had ensured he'd know my taste for the rest of the day.

But this was not how this morning was going to go.

After gratuitous yet tender kisses, Nelly turned around in my arms so he was facing away from me. One day, I'd just go between his thighs and enjoy that simpler friction, but not yet, not when being inside him was too tempting by a mile.

I grabbed his hip hard and went about getting him slick. I did that very slowly, and he whined and trembled, not a reaction humans typically had to sex magic. Average humans wouldn't be able to feel the magic as it did what it did, only mages might be able to detect this intrusive spellwork.

But even in this simple thing, Nelly made it clear he was more than a mage, more than a necromancer or even a human. What a fool I had been to miss it for such a long time.

When I was done, I worked him open, taking my time. He was gazing at my wings, the left one stretched over him in a protective way that had been unconscious on my part. So long as the feathers enchanted him, I'd call it good.

He braided the fingers of one hand with mine, maybe so he wouldn't be tempted to touch my wings, and I was willing to not mind that reluctance for once because it meant he was holding on to me.

And he was ready now. His small, hitching breaths fanned against my arm as I lifted his leg so I could push into his heat. How the experience was this good every single time I had no idea, but he was so tight around me, very slick now that I had made him so, and every little tremor, every almost moan, told me he loved it.

Loved how I possessed him in this moment, loved how I claimed him. Loved me.

The act itself was a linear thing. I moved in a steady

rhythm though I would not allow him to touch his own, straining cock. There was truly nothing special about the mechanics of this.

It was the way he felt, his thoughts, the swooping, swaying, all-encompassing realization that we were meant to be—each other's, together forever, one.

And he was right to feel like freefalling, because it was a startling thought, to own and be owned, to want and be wanted. I would have him always, just like he would have me. The world—kingdoms, republics, whole civilizations—could go ahead and crumble to dust or destroy themselves, but it wouldn't matter, because during the worst of it and at the end of everything, he would be there, his golden eyes looking into mine and assuring me that he was still here with me.

I came hard, bone-shattering, blood-boiling, mind-bogglingly deep and hard, and Nelly, my perfect other, came untouched, all his thoughts scattering so that all I could pick up with my wings was just bliss, maybe a few colors here and there, stars and rainbows.

"I love you," I whispered into his ear after we'd not moved for a long while. I felt him smile before he pressed his lips against my open palm and returned the words to me in a low whisper.

✦

NELLY INSISTED ON being properly dressed, and then he had grumbled about the nice golden-brown sweater I'd gotten for him because it was extremely soft. He'd succumbed though, but he could not be convinced to head to the great room before stopping by the kitchen.

"Need coffee," he grumbled.

"Hmm, maybe we should do another juice cleanse to kick the new year off?" I said as we walked through one of the older parts of the castle where painted wooden beams had been carefully restored.

Nelly gave me the cutest, most evil glare. "No fucking juice cleanse ever again, do you fucking hear me, Beelzebug? I swear it would be the straw that breaks my willingness to perform sexual favors for you."

I chuckled. "Favors?" Ah, he needed to be edged again soon. He was always less cheeky after a long night of being denied.

"You heard me. No fucking juice cleanse, I'm serious."

The kitchen was abandoned, but it looked like Sephy and Hades had been there to get breakfast ready. The coffee maker had a second pot waiting, and Nelly made a beeline for it. I leaned on the counter in front of the cabinet with the mugs, and he did a little more of that adorable glaring.

"Mug, Beelzebug. Gimme."

"What do you say?"

He bit his lip in the most seductive way, teeth clenching with the desire to spit something sarcastic at me. But then he said, "Please."

And like that, I was considering whether I could possibly convince him to show me the bathroom again.

I turned and got a mug out for him. "Here you go, babe."

"Thanks," he mumbled and filled it almost to the brim, took a long gulp, and sighed happily.

"Did you want to get coffee so you could avoid unwrapping presents?"

He shrugged and looked at the contents of his mug. "We can go and do presents now."

Personally, I couldn't wait.

"FINALLY," TRONY SAID. The angel was dressed for the day, wearing leggings with a Santa print under a red dress with white fake fur trim.

"Yes, finally," Tiamat chimed in. "The snow is very nice, albeit deep. It's not a day to be stuck inside."

Hades, however, was completely distracted by Soul and her babies. "We did not get anything for the wee ones," he said.

Sephy giggled. "Give them cuddles. Pumpkin, come over here and sit with me. We have fruit cake and biscuits as well as scones." She patted the couch next to her.

I gave Nelly a gentle push when he decided to be shy for no good reason. Cerberus, for once, was watching Soul and his babies instead of the fruit cake. A Midwinter Miracle.

"I'm going first," I said before Trony could master-of-ceremony the unwrapping.

For today, I'd gotten my necromancer two gifts, and I picked out the smaller one first. The wrapping was a pure shimmery black paper, and it had a black bow. Nelly eyed it a little suspiciously when I sat on the couch next to him and held it out for him to take.

"Blessed Saturnalia-Yule-Holiday mashup, my love," I said.

After not all that long, he put his coffee down and went to town on the wrapping paper like the wide-eyed child he had never been allowed to be.

He paused briefly before opening the black satin box inside, but then said, "Oh."

Sephy leaned a little closer and elbowed him in the

ribs. "See? I told you that you needed your ears pierced."

"Mmm. I agree although that makes this very nearly a last-minute present," I said.

Nelly was still looking at the sapphire ear studs even as Hades came over, Quincey in his arms.

"Aye, these're pretty. They will look good on you, lad."

"Very," the dragon mother agreed. "Now, let's keep this unwrapping business moving before all the snow melts."

And no one argued with the dragon mother.

Trony took charge and simply went about distributing boxes all around.

The first one we all opened were identical boxes from Tiamat that easily fit into your palm.

"Oh, candy?" Nelly asked. He looked at the single praline in his box. This year's ones were very pretty, mostly dark chocolate and topped with blue flowers that looked like they had just been plucked.

"Yes, candy. A taste of something that is very special to you," Tiamat explained.

"Let's all eat them now," Sephy said. "On three."

She counted, and on three, we all put the praline into our mouths. I let it sit on my tongue for a moment because I was pretty sure what taste I would get this year, and yes, there it was. Grapes, fresh and still warm from the sun, hinting at what their wine would taste like.

I bit into the chocolate, and the flavor of the rich young wine exploded in my mouth, much stronger than I'd ever tasted, but as strong as I had no doubt it would be someday. As strong as I knew my Nelly was.

I had no idea what Nelly tasted, but he looked amazed, mouth slack, pupils slightly wide.

"Shoes!" the dragon mother said when she got to the present Nelly and I had selected for her, and Nelly was pulled back to the now.

"Babe, can I put your new earrings on you?" I asked as all around, paper was being torn.

"More shoes!" the dragon mother said when she'd unwrapped Hades and Sephy's gift.

"O-okay. But be careful? Dolly said not to take them out for a while."

"Don't worry sweet. Who is Dolly?"

He shrugged. "The stylist who couldn't wait to punch a needle through me."

"Mmm. I should thank her. But this will be fine. I have a steady hand."

"Aye, steady at picking from the bottom shelf," Hades said and raised the indeed quite cheap whiskey bottle I had picked out for him toward us. "Watch here, Quincey, this is what we do not drink. It's what we use to kill mold and disinfect wounds." Hades showed Quincey the bottle, although unlike his sister, this hellpuppy was still blind.

"Oh, not this again," Sephy said.

"And more shoes! Aww!" Tiamat said after unwrapping what Trony had gotten her.

I replaced the first stud. The small puncture had mostly healed already, but I was still careful when I put the new earring in, then did the second one. Nelly held his head still, his hands on my sides.

"Not what again, Sephy?" Nelly asked.

Sephy rolled her eyes. "These two give each other cheap liquor and cheap knick-knacks—"

"Lass, don't you go spoil what I got Lucy."

Sephy rolled her eyes again and tore into her next

present just when I closed the second earring. "Cheap whatevers each year. There is a collection in an upstairs room, bottles from all over, and probably all of them disgusting."

My necromancer grinned. "It's kind of cool though."

I turned his head from side to side. "You look kind of cool, my love. So very beautiful."

"Let me see," Sephy said and stood. After a moment, she nodded and gave Nelly two thumbs up, which made him smile. "Yup, they do make you look beautiful. And kind of cool too."

Kind of cool was also what my little, secretive corpse raiser had given Hades and Sephy, who hugged him hard when she'd unwrapped her oven mitts.

"Handling hot stuff year-round?" Hades quipped when he was allowed to examine said mitts. He'd put Quincey back with his mom and sister because the wrapping paper that was piling up around us was a potential choking hazard for a little hellbaby.

I was turning what Hades had given me over, a weird little rubber giraffe. "Not you. Casseroles and such."

"Mate, are you needing your cock handed to you in yet another snowball fight?"

"No fighting, you two," Tiamat commanded. "I don't need you making a ruckus when I go snowbathing."

I was not so sure she would make it outside though. She'd put her three pairs of shoes out in a neat row on the table in front of her and was now cooing at each pair in turn.

"Oh!" Trony said, followed by the telltale noise of a crop hitting a palm. "This is wonderful."

"Am I forgiven for your floors?" I asked.

"Uhm, he means are we forgiven. It's from both of

us," Nelly said.

Trony beamed, which was a rare sight. She waved the pink riding crop around as if to test how flexible it was. "This one time. But only because I have an ass in mind who I'll try this out on very soon."

"Not information I needed," Nelly said and held up a bottle to Hades. "Thank you for this, but what exactly is it? It just says Mimir's."

I snorted. "You didn't seriously brew that for my Nelly, did you?"

"Oh, you bet I did. It's truth serum, simply put." Hades, the ass, pointed at me. "If you can get it in him, he'll give you straight answers to any question you ask him, none of the paraphrasing and prevaricating shite he loves so much."

"I am usually direct," I said.

Sephy leaned toward Nelly and whispered in a conspiratorial voice, "This is where it starts."

"You need a lesson. Dragon mother, I beg of you, one challenge to teach the Devil a lesson," Hades said.

Tiamat looked at the zebra print stilettos Hades and Sephy had given her and ran one finger lovingly along the heel.

"Fine. But no unnecessary screaming."

"Aye. All the screaming he will do will be needed," Hades said, not knowing I was going to shove a snowball where it would make *him* scream.

"Right after we are done here," I said, and Hades nodded, then proceeded to the next gift.

Once he had it unwrapped, Nelly very quickly found himself hugged tight all over again. I personally did not see why a *Best Magic Teacher* mug was so special.

"Thank you, lad. I'll cherish these," Hades said,

looking a bit gooey around his usually hard face as he looked from the mug to a set of tumblers with the same engraving.

With Nelly happily flustered after that—and Hades moving his tea from the regular cup to his new one—I thought it was time to hand my necromancer his second gift.

"Yours, babe. From me."

He took the larger box, which was wrapped like the first.

"You didn't have to give me anything else," he said and gave the box a small shake. Then he tore through the black wrapping paper with a smile on his face.

This gift, I had not gotten him as late as the earrings, and it was not only made to order, but imbued with my magic on top of that.

Nelly opened the box I had selected for this and stared at the black plug. It was a bit larger than the ones he'd gotten used to, and it came with a few other extras, though those were not obvious, and it would have to be inside him for him to experience.

"Now that's not a bottom shelf bottle of liquor," Sephy said, leaning over to him.

Nelly turned red and shut the box quickly. "Guess not." He turned to me. "Couldn't give me this later, could you?"

"I wanted you to see it."

"I bet you did."

"Nothing wrong with a nice thick dildo, in my book, and I am—the Best Magic Teacher," Hades said and held his mug up for us all to see. I dearly hoped this would not turn into a habit.

Trony's gift to me was a pair of socks, very nice

ones, and her way of telling me something, although I was still not quite sure, after all these years of being given socks, what that was. Sephy had found me several vintage postcards of nude Victorians in strange poses only Victorians could find sexy. She liked the holiday decorations I had given her, turning each one over and examining it closely.

And my necromancer—well. His gift was not what I had expected. "Babe," I said as I turned on the e-reader. In a Devil-positive chibi sleeve. "Babe. Oh my."

"You like it?" he asked, voice filled with uncertainty.

"Babe, I love it!" I pulled him into my arms. "But I know you like to read the summaries on the back of my books. Hmm. Maybe I should start reading you the highlights? Or my favorite scenes? There was this one in the book I read the other day where they were playing chase and—"

"Nope, no. Thanks. I'm all good."

"But babe, in that other book, there was that vampire who'd just been woken from being imprisoned for decades, and he got the one who freed him to—"

"Nope, I don't need that information."

"Ah, young love and old reading habits," Tiamat said. "I think I will try them all on. In a little while." She tapped each one of her new shoes in turn.

That was good because it meant I could take my time snowball fighting Hades later on.

"Are we all done?" Sephy asked.

"One more." I pulled up a book I knew and swiped straight to where I remembered a good scene started, then handed the e-reader to Nelly before opening the last box. Which was, going by a first peek, possibly better than the e-reader.

Lionel

I READ ONE PARAGRAPH, BUT AT THE MENTION OF A BARBED monster cock, I discreetly stopped and looked at the large, if flat, box Lucifer had unwrapped. Then, my phone chirped.

I pulled it out and read the message from Metatron: *That's the alternative gift from you he's unwrapping btw. Thank you SO MUCH for the riding crop!*

I smiled over at Trony, who was waving her riding crop back at me. She'd gotten pink handcuffs and a cute pink dress as well. I wondered how all those things went together, but not enough to actually ask her about it.

My attention was drawn back to Lucifer when he pulled the lid of this second present open.

"Babe," he said, voice full of stunned admiration.

I didn't immediately comprehend, because the contents were Christmas-themed in color, but...

My face heated. There was one mask, red with tinsel and stars, and a blindfold in the same design. And there was a...well, it had feathers and could have been a cat toy, except I wasn't that naive. And the candy cane colored thing... I watched porn, so I knew it was an anal hook, but...it was over the top, wasn't it, given there was also a dildo in the approximate shape of a Christmas tree, complete with ridges. And velvet ribbon for gift wrapping of the kinky kind.

What in the ever-living fuck had Metatron been thinking? Then again, handcuffs, riding crop, and cute pink dress. It was pretty clear what she'd been thinking.

Tiamat peered over. "I suppose some seasonally themed presents are acceptable. This one most certainly is."

"Babe," Lucifer said again and turned to me. He was smiling like a cat getting ready to play with each and every single thing inside that box, and with me, the accidental canary.

"Uhm, that's actually more from Trony than me," I managed.

"Nonsense. I take no credit for it," Metatron, the traitorous angel, said.

"You are not getting to play with your new toys now." Persephone, my savior, was the best, pulling me to my feet and out of Lucifer's reach. The Devil followed me with his eyes, a lot like a cat who wanted to sink his claws into that new toy.

"Aye, everyone, come along now," Hades said, and before I knew what was going on, Lucifer had put the box aside, not that he'd closed it or anything. No, all the sex toys were left out and on full display.

At least, Tiamat was the only one still in her bathrobe. Everyone else was dressed head to toe, something that surprised me, which completely failed to raise any concerns. The side effects of dating a god really should have been printed somewhere on Lucifer's gorgeous body somewhere.

Cerberus scampered along as well, all three heads looking eager.

"What's happening?" I asked.

"Well, pumpkin, I got you something as well, but I

didn't want to put it under the tree," Persephone said.

"You didn't have to do that," I said. "You already got me the makeover." I pointed to my new hair and the new earrings.

"That was nothing, pumpkin."

We went through the kitchen and from there to the hallway on the right. The mudroom was past the vegetable garden door, and Lucifer was quick to help me into my coat while Hades helped Persephone into her jacket.

Tiamat was taking her bathrobe off, and I tried telling myself that all that nakedness was just a new normal and that she would turn into a dragon soon anyway, and that it would be ridiculous for a dragon to wear a bathrobe.

"Ah, we should have brought the sexy blindfold," Persephone said when she zipped up her jacket.

"What?"

Lucifer was next to me and busy with coiling the scarf around my neck. He chuckled. "No need. I'll take care of it."

His wings appeared and pulled me in, close to him.

"Can't stand not being in the spotlight for five minutes, can you," Hades said.

Lucifer, after pulling me close, gave a derisive snort. "The spotlight is just drawn to me naturally. But maybe you will get some more attention as well when you lose against me later. Or wait, is it still called attention when it's pity?"

"Hah, ye—"

"Save it," Persephone said, and we were moving.

"Excited, babe?" Lucifer asked.

"What's happening?" I was losing the sense of where we were going, although I felt and smelled the cold air outside, and snow was still coming down, though not as much as yesterday. A few snowflakes sailed past the shelter of Lucifer's wings.

"You'll see."

"Wait, you know what this is?"

"He knows what this is?" Persephone echoed, sounding stern.

"Lass, it came up. But you know Lucy. Never lies but misplaces the truth anyway. Which is what the Mimir's is for, lad, don't you forget that."

"Mimir's water is also quite delicious if mixed with fresh spring water," Tiamat added.

A thought hit me, and I was glad for the shelter of Lucifer's wings. "I'm not being tossed into a well, am I?"

"I'm not allowed to," Hades said. "Don't ye hold it against my Best Magic Teacher reputation, lad."

"Nope, that reputation is unshakable," I said, glad the well wasn't happening, for now.

I recognized the sound of the stable doors being pulled open, and of course the greeting neighs and the smell of the horses were unmistakable.

"This way," Persephone said. "Nelly, close your eyes so Lucy can put his wings away."

I did and felt Lucifer's feathers brush over my cheek.

Quite truthfully, I wasn't sure what to make of today. Last night had been long, but also so much fun. I'd never thought that having a party with a bunch of gods would be that much fun, but it truly had been, and the way Lucifer had helped me with the geese and had made sure they would be taken care of and safe for the rest of their lives just made me feel like the marketing hoax of Holiday Spirit was a real thing after all.

And the presents. That had been so awkward at first because…I wasn't sure what was expected of me in terms of showing gratitude. I was more thankful than I knew how to adequately express. Hades and Persephone had somehow ended up just accepting me as part of the family. The dragon mother had pretty much done the very same from the first moment I'd met her, even if I'd only realized it later on.

And Metatron, the angel who cared. She had been acerbic and abrasive to varying degrees—still was—and she was never shy about sharing an opinion, but fuck, she'd redone my old apartment. She'd always made sure I had coffee in the morning. She might have been a tough angel cookie, but she did care, not because she had to, but because she chose to do so.

Which was humbling, especially because it was unexpected. To find all that in these gods, who sounded like different people if you listened to the myths about them.

"Okay, one more step. Yup. And I'm just going to turn you a little, pumpkin. Okay, that's it. Now open your eyes."

I did but didn't quite comprehend.

In front of me, staring back at me, stood a horse with large eyes and ears that were bigger than those of the other horses I'd gotten to know. The horse's coat was a solid, glossy black, and its wings were the same shimmery darkness.

Because yeah, that horse had wings.

"That…that's a pegasus," I said, and the pegasus's ears twitched when I spoke. No one else was saying anything, I realized, but they were all looking into the stable through the bars above the wooden stable walls.

"He is," Persephone said. She was standing off to the side, though she was in the stable as well, a wide smile on her face. "His name's Toffee."

The pegasus looked at her when she said his name. "Toffee?"

The pegasus looked right back at me and took a tentative step my way. All the horses I had met here at the castle were smart in their own way, but the pegasus definitely had intelligent eyes. He came another step closer, and I held out my hand.

After one more step from him, I saw his nostrils move, meaning he was probably getting my scent. Stupidly, it reminded me of Lucifer.

The pegasus came touching-close, and I ran my fingers over his silky soft nose. He neighed. "Hi there, Toffee."

"Well done, lad," Hades said. "Ain't just anyone who can befriend a pegasus at first try and make them their own."

Lucifer growled, and I could see him through the bars giving Hades a dirty sideways look.

"Did you think any pegasus worth their wings would reject my Nelly?"

Toffee turned toward them but stepped closer again, so I started scratching his ears like I knew most of the other horses liked.

"They are just being big, silly alpha gods," I said, and Toffee looked at me as if he were listening. Then Hades' words registered. "Wait, make him mine you said, Hades?"

Persephone answered instead. "He is yours. My Midwinter gift to you. And of course I will teach you how to properly ride him."

I looked at her and my jaw dropped. "You got me a pegasus? For Christmas?"

She shrugged. "Yes."

"But Sephy, that's, I mean. Thank you. I can't even... thank you."

I hesitated, but then left Toffee standing there in order to give Persephone a hug. It just felt right.

She patted my back. "You are very welcome, pumpkin. But I expect you here on the weekends to take care of him. Pegasi are fussy about that sort of thing, and they don't really like people unless they are their people."

"I will, of course." I turned back to Toffee. "What do you think? Am I your people?"

He tilted his head as if he were trying to make out what I was saying. I had no idea if he understood, or if he did, then how much of it, but either way, he walked back toward me, and then, careful but certain, he booped my nose with his.

"So lovely when they form a bond," the dragon mother said.

"They can be super prickly, but at least this one keeps his wings clean," Metatron said, because she was an angel with priorities.

"Now that this is done…Hades, I challenge you."

"Mate, I challenged you first."

Hades and Lucifer disappeared from the side of the stable, and I saw them strip through the open stable door.

"You've got to be kidding me," I said and looked at Toffee. "I'm sorry that you have to go through this."

The pegasus tilted his head and neighed curiously.

"Do you think I can feed him a carrot?" I asked Persephone.

We'd followed Hades and Lucifer outside. The castle's courtyard was properly buried, and even the path that hugged close to the castle wall and led to the stables had a good four inches again. But at least the sun was finally breaking through the thick cloud cover now.

Toffee did not seem to mind at all and flapped his raven wings in the flurrying flakes. Just like Persephone had said, the pegasus had gamely followed me.

Our alpha gods, meanwhile, had stripped their clothes off in the stables and were now out there in the snow, not that I could see them. It was for the better. I did not need to see the Best Magic Teacher's naked ass while he tossed snowballs at my boyfriend.

"Of course you can, pumpkin."

"I'll get you carrots," Metatron said and teleported away.

"If she gets the carrots, I'll make us some tea so we don't freeze while we watch our alpha gods," Persephone said and walked back toward the castle's entrance.

The dragon mother came to stand next to me and sighed. "I think I will go back inside. To try on the shoes." She leaned over and kissed me on the forehead. I was never sure whether it was always magic with Tiamat or whether it was just her, but calm flooded me, and everything else—especially the sight of naked gods around me—suddenly mattered less, suddenly didn't matter at all.

Instead, calm settled in, the calm that came from knowing who you were and who your people were. Toffee neighed on my other side and rubbed his head against my shoulder.

"Treat each other well," the dragon mother said. "A pegasus will rise above the clouds and dive to hell for his rider, or so the saying goes. Always remember that when you get on his back, young one."

"I will." I patted Toffee's muscular neck.

"Good," the dragon mother said and walked back to the castle.

Metatron appeared a second later and wordlessly handed me a bunch of carrots. I held out one, and Toffee took a careful bite.

"See what this does for your pretty hair," I heard Hades shout out.

"Unadulterated idiocy," Metatron said.

"They know we can't see them from here, right?"

She shrugged.

Lucifer's laughter rang over the snow. "You think that's all it takes to vanquish me? I will teach you, oh Bestest Teacher of Magic."

"Mate, do not abuse the title."

Persephone came back outside with a thermos and three mugs. "Has anyone bothered telling them we cannot see them from here?"

"Nah," Metatron said.

"No," I said.

Toffee neighed and eyed the thermos with interest, so I held out another carrot to him.

"I suppose it serves them right," Persephone said.

"Like either of you will tell them anything other than what good fighters they are when they're done with that nonsense," Metatron said.

Persephone and I exchanged a look before we smiled together. This was what it meant to own an alpha god and be owned by them in turn—sometimes you would lie to them, even if they could not lie. If anything, I hoped it would make Lucy love me even more. Because deep down, I knew that he would never love me less.

The End

Lucy and Nelly will return.

AND THE STORY IS DONE...
FOR NOW.

If you enjoyed this small adventure Lucy and Nelly had together, it would mean the world to me if you could take a moment and leave a review on Goodreads and wherever you bought *A Devilish Saturnalia*. It helps get this book into the hands of more readers, and that helps me write more books.

Thank you!
Alexa Piper

Goodreads

Where to find *A Devilish Saturnalia*

ABOUT ALEXA PIPER

Alexa (she/her) has a lot of characters living in her head and wanting their stories told. Many of these people get snarky and won't stop complaining if Alexa is too slow writing them, which means that for this author, sleep is a luxury. Consequently, Alexa is a coffee addict, but she is sure she has it under control (six cups of coffee are normal in a morning, right? Right!?)

Never miss anything Alexa does and join her newsletter.